PRAISE F

a time of miracles

WINNER OF THE MILDRED L. BATCHELDER AWARD
(for an outstanding children's book originally published in a foreign language)
AN ALA-YALSA BEST FICTION FOR YOUNG ADULTS BOOK
AN ALA-ALSC NOTABLE CHILDREN'S BOOK
A CCBC CHOICES BOOK

★ "An exceptional story."
—*School Library Journal*, Starred

★ "A beautifully cadenced tribute to maternal love and
the power of stories amid contemporary political chaos."
—*Kirkus Reviews*, Starred

★ "[A] beautifully nuanced novel."
—*Publishers Weekly*, Starred

★ "Readers will find themselves mesmerized
not only by the eloquent language but by a plot
every bit as harrowing and surprising as
Koumaïl's cherished bedtime story."
—*The Horn Book Magazine*, Starred

Also by Anne-Laure Bondoux

The Killer's Tears
A Mildred L. Batchelder Honor Book
(for an outstanding children's book originally published in a foreign language)
Life As It Comes
Vasco, Leader of the Tribe
The Destiny of Linus Hoppe
The Second Life of Linus Hoppe

anne-laure bondoux

a time of miracles

TRANSLATED FROM THE FRENCH BY Y. MAUDET

EMBER

Text copyright © 2009 by Bayard Éditions Jeunesse
Translation copyright © 2010 by Y. Maudet
Map illustration copyright © 2010 by Rick Britton
Cover photograph copyright © 2010 by Jessica Boone/Getty Images

Visit us on the Web! randomhouse.com/teens

Educators and librarians, for a variety of teaching tools,
visit us at RHTeachersLibrarians.com

The Library of Congress has cataloged the hardcover edition of this work as follows:
Bondoux, Anne-Laure.
[Temps des miracles English]
A time of miracles / Anne-Laure Bondoux ; translated from the French
by Y. Maudet. — 1st ed. p. cm.
Summary: In the early 1990s, a boy with a mysterious past and the woman who cares for him endure a five-year journey across the war-torn Caucasus and Europe, weathering hardships and welcoming unforgettable encounters with other refugees searching for a better life.
ISBN 978-0-385-73922-1 (hardcover : alk. paper) — ISBN 978-0-375-89726-9 (ebook) —
ISBN 978-0-385-90777-4 (Gibraltar lib. bdg. : alk. paper) [1. Refugees—Fiction.
2. War—Fiction. 3. Secrets—Fiction. 4. Survival—Fiction.
5. Caucasus—History—20th century—Fiction. 6. Europe—History—20th century—Fiction.]
I. Maudet, Y. II. Title.
PZ7.B63696Ti 2010
[Fic]—dc22
2010008539

ISBN 978-0-375-86036-2 (tr. pbk.)

RL: 5.5

Printed in the United States of America

10 9 8 7 6 5 4 3 2

First Ember Edition 2012

Random House Children's Books supports the First Amendment
and celebrates the right to read.

For my mother

a time of miracles

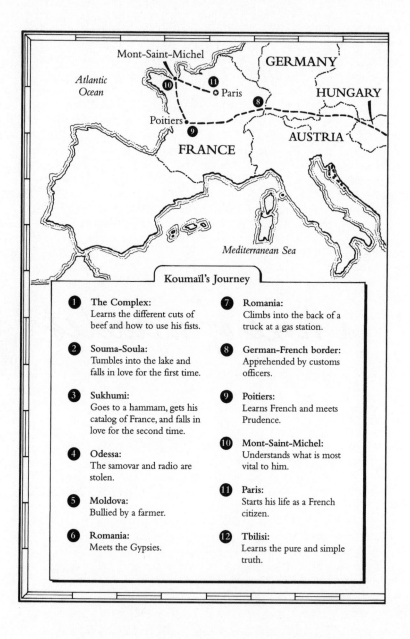

Koumaïl's Journey

1 The Complex:
Learns the different cuts of beef and how to use his fists.

2 Souma-Soula:
Tumbles into the lake and falls in love for the first time.

3 Sukhumi:
Goes to a hammam, gets his catalog of France, and falls in love for the second time.

4 Odessa:
The samovar and radio are stolen.

5 Moldova:
Bullied by a farmer.

6 Romania:
Meets the Gypsies.

7 Romania:
Climbs into the back of a truck at a gas station.

8 German-French border:
Apprehended by customs officers.

9 Poitiers:
Learns French and meets Prudence.

10 Mont-Saint-Michel:
Understands what is most vital to him.

11 Paris:
Starts his life as a French citizen.

12 Tbilisi:
Learns the pure and simple truth.

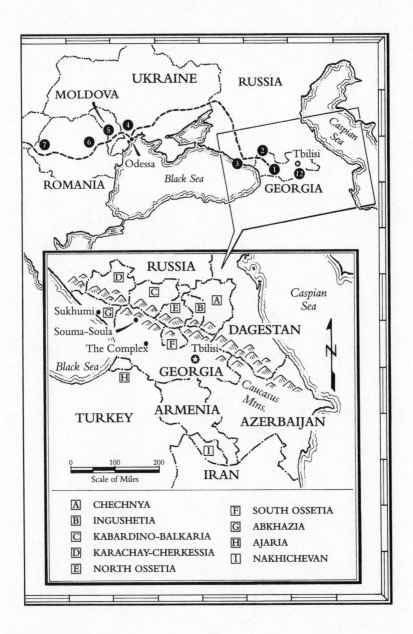

chapter one

MY name is Blaise Fortune and I am a citizen of the French Republic. It's the pure and simple truth.

I was almost twelve years old the day the customs officers found me in the back of the truck. I stank as badly as the garbage shed where Abdelmalik slept, and all I was able to say was "Mynameisblaisefortuneandiamacitizenofthefrench-republicitsthepureandsimpletruth."

I had lost nearly all of my precious belongings along the way. Fortunately, I still had my passport; Gloria had made sure to stick it deep in my jacket pocket when we were at the service station. My passport proved that I was born on December 28, 1985, at Mont-Saint-Michel, on the French side of the English Channel, per page 16 of the green atlas. It was written in black and white. The problem was my photo: it had been removed, then glued back, and even though Mr. Ha had faked the official seal with the greatest care, the customs officers didn't believe that I was really a

French boy. I wanted to explain my story to them, but I didn't have the vocabulary. So they pulled me out of the truck by the neck of my sweater and took me away.

This is how my childhood ended: brutally, on the side of a highway, when I realized that Gloria had disappeared and that I would have to cope without her in the country known for human rights and for the poetry of Charles Baudelaire.

After that I spent countless days in a triage zone, then in a shelter. France was just a succession of walls, fences, and doors. I slept in dormitories that reminded me of the Matachine's attic, except that there was no dormer window to watch the stars through. I was alone in the world. But I couldn't let despair eat away at my soul. More so than ever, I had to go to Mont-Saint-Michel to find my mother! It was easy to explain it all, but I didn't know the language. I couldn't give details about the Terrible Accident or the hazards of life that had brought me here. And when you can't express yourself, it's like dying of suffocation.

Things are different today. Many years have gone by, and now I can name everything; I can conjugate verbs, use adjectives and conjunctions. I have a new passport in my pocket—all in good order, as required by the laws of the world.

Not long ago I received a letter from the French Embassy in Tbilisi, Georgia, saying that they might have tracked down Gloria. That's why I'm sitting at a Charles de Gaulle Airport gate with a suitcase, a heart that beats madly, and the crazy hope that I will see Gloria again. But, before anything else, I must put my thoughts in order.

Let me begin: My name is Blaise Fortune. I am a citizen

of the French Republic, even though I spent the first eleven years of my life in the Caucasus, a vast region located between the Black Sea and the Caspian Sea, per page 78 of the green atlas. At the time I spoke Russian and people called me Koumaïl. It might seem strange, but it's easy to understand. I just have to tell my story. All of it. And in the right order.

chapter two

MY oldest memories date back to 1992, when Gloria and I lived in the Complex with other refugee families. I don't remember the name of the town. I am nearly seven. It is winter, and we no longer have electricity or heat because of the war.

There is a smell of laundry mingled with that of vinegar.

Women are gathered in the center of the courtyard, around a huge iron vat set above blazing logs. The skin on their bare arms is red up to the elbows. They speak and laugh loudly. As the laundry boils in the scum of our dirt, a cloud of steam rises, leaving a thick condensation on the window-panes of the floors above.

Farther away, under the canopy, creepy Sergei sharpens his razor. *Schlick, schlick, schlick.*

He calls us over, one by one.

"You! Come here!" he hollers.

Creepy Sergei doesn't know our names. There are too

many kids in the Complex, and he drinks so heavily that his memory is completely shot. He just yells, "You," as he points his razor at one of us. Nobody dares disobey him, because we're terrified of his upturned eye and his flattened nose.

Before becoming a barber, creepy Sergei was a boxer, the best one in town, or so they say. But everything changed the day a high-strung Armenian knocked him out cold. It was before the war. According to Gloria, on that day Sergei had a brush with death. That makes him special now, and he deserves our respect. So when he points his razor at me, I dash under the canopy.

I sit on the three-legged stool, my back turned to him, my heart beating madly, and I lean my head back. Sergei's razor cuts across my scalp, his strokes methodical, until all my hair falls to the ground. Then creepy Sergei dips a towel in a barrel of vinegar and rubs my head with it. My scalp stings. I whine. He pushes me from the stool.

"Go see your mother, little brat!" he says.

I stand up, my head shorn and filled with a vague pain, and I rush to snuggle in Gloria's arms. She's not my mother, but she's all I have.

"Beautiful!" she exclaims as she runs her soapy hands over my skull.

I look up at her and she bends down to kiss my cheek. "You're truly magnificent, Monsieur Blaise," she adds.

I smile through my tears. I love it when she calls me "Mr. Blaise" in French, because no one else can understand.

"Now go and play, Koumaïl," she says loudly. "You can see I'm busy!"

I dry my eyes and run off to join the group of shaved kids who are playing in the courtyard.

The laundry, the laughter, the razor, the vinegar . . . that's how we wage war against lice, fleas, and all forms of parasites—including, according to Gloria, the most feared parasite of all, despair. Despair, she says, is more dangerous and more clever than the Armenian who knocked out Sergei. It is invisible and slips into everything. If you don't fight against it, it nibbles at your soul. But how do you know you've caught a despair if you can't even see it? I wonder. What do you do if even the razor can't get rid of it? Gloria holds me tight against her chest when I ask her about this. She explains that she has a cure.

"As long as you stay close to me, nothing bad will happen to you, OK?"

"OK."

chapter three

THE Complex is a group of three buildings that form a U around a courtyard. Gloria and I have a room on the second floor.

I can take six steps from one wall to another, going around the wood-burning stove. The wallpaper is coming loose, and behind it the paint is chipping. When I scratch the plaster with my nail, the bricks appear. The Complex is full of cracks—totally eaten away by the dampness that seeps up from the ground because it's built near a river. It's so rotten that it was supposed to be demolished, but the war stopped the bulldozers; now it's our refuge, a good hiding place that protects us from the wind and the militia.

I'm very familiar with the wind: it blows down from the mountains as fast as an avalanche and rushes under doors to freeze you to the bone. But I have no idea what the militia is. All I know is that it scares me even more than Sergei's upturned eye, and that everybody here has some reason to be wary of it. That's why we've set up rotating shifts of people who keep watch: night after night, teams of four take turns watching the entrance to the Complex. Kids can hang around only if the grown-ups allow them to.

I was told that if I see men wearing boots, if I see their leather jackets and their clubs, I'm supposed to rush into the courtyard and pull hard on the bell that's suspended under the canopy.

There are three other times when we're supposed to ring the bell with all our might:

1. If the Complex is on fire
2. If the Complex starts to crumble down
3. If the Psezkaya River is overflowing

Except under these circumstances, no one is to touch the bell. If you do, you'll be immediately expelled from the Complex.

When I ask Gloria what the militia would do if it were to catch us, her face hardens and I regret my question.

"A seven-year-old boy doesn't need to know everything," she tells me. "Just be satisfied following the rules, Koumaïl."

I nod and go off to play with the others in the stairwell. Depending on our mood, the staircase becomes our fortress or our warship.

My playmates are Emil, Baksa, Rebeka, Tasmin, and Faïna. They are thin and lice-ridden, as supple as eels. Some speak Russian like me, others not, but children don't need words to understand each other. We run until we're out of breath. We sprint up and down the stairs. We hide in the toilets, or behind the sheets that are drying on the roof, all the better to scare old Mrs. Hanska. Our laughter echoes throughout the Complex, from top to bottom, faster than any draft.

Gloria says that she likes to hear me laugh, that laughter is the most important thing in the world.

I like to hear Gloria laughing too. But Gloria also coughs, which I don't like to hear. Coughing makes her turn purple, and she loses her breath; I have the impression that a great big dog is barking inside her chest. I'm no doctor, but it's not hard to guess that her cough sounds deadly. What would happen if Gloria were to die? I worry.

"Tsk, tsk, tsk!" she says, and laughs when her coughing fit ends. "Don't look so gloomy. You're not burying me yet, Monsieur Blaise! You know very well that I'm as sturdy as the trees. Now come on, Koumaïl! Go and fetch us some water if you want to eat tonight!"

I hurry with the bucket to the hose in the courtyard. I'm always ready to help or to do somebody a favor because I'm in a rush to grow up. I sense that the world in which we live is hostile to children. I dream of the day when my legs will be long enough that I can run very fast, and when I will be strong enough to carry the khaki canvas bag that Gloria calls our "gear."

Ever since we've lived in the Complex, the gear has been put away on a shelf just above the door. For the time being, it contains only the tin box where Gloria hides her secrets, and I am not allowed to open it.

Everything else we have is scattered in the room—our clothes, my green atlas, the blankets, the basic cooking utensils, the stringless violin, the radio, and Vassili's samovar to make tea. If I ever hear the bell ring, I know what to do: climb on a chair, grab the gear, and stuff it with our belongings as fast as I can. Sometimes I train mentally for this emergency—the chair, the gear, the belongings—and I imagine how the Complex will empty itself of its occupants as quickly as a draining bathtub. I ask Gloria what we would do next.

She shrugs. "Exactly what we've done so far, Koumaïl," she says. "We will walk straight in front of us toward a new horizon."

"OK."

In the Complex everybody has a story to tell. Whether it's about earthquakes, collapsed mines, jail terms, poker games in shady ports, childbirths, separations, or reunions. Even Old Max will tell you how he lost three of his fingers when he worked in a slaughterhouse. Everything is new to me; I ask endless questions and I learn fast, but no story fascinates me more than my own, especially when Gloria whispers it in my ear before I go to sleep at night.

"Again?" she asks while putting a log in the stove.

"Yes, again! Don't leave anything out!" I say.

She sits on the bed. Her face moves in the flickering light of the stove. She pulls the lambskin blanket up to my nose.

"It was the end of summer, and I lived with my father, old Vassili, in his home," she begins.

"The one who gave you the samovar?"

"Yes, Koumaïl. At that time Vassili owned the most

beautiful orchard in all of the Caucasus. You should have seen the apple trees, pear trees, apricot trees—acres upon acres covered with trees! With the river on one side and the railroad track on the other."

"That's where you used to walk with Zemzem!"

A fire lights up in Gloria's eyes. "Hold on, you're going too fast. I always tell things properly, in the right order, you know that."

I take hold of one of her hands and keep quiet. I listen to my story. In the right order.

chapter four

OLD Vassili has a long, tapered mustache and wears a pair of suspenders solidly attached to his pants. When he smiles, his mustache tickles his ears, and when he raises his arms to the sky, the suspenders pull up his pants so high that you can see his hairy calves.

Vassili doesn't smile often. Instead, several times a day, he raises his arms to the sky because life causes him so many worries. He yells at the whole world, but mostly at his workers.

"Hurry up, you bunch of clumsy toads! Easy with the peaches! Gentle with the apricots! And fix the truck before my anger strikes you like lightning!"

Workers bustle about until Vassili curls his mustache and rubs his ulcerated stomach, gripped by his next worry.

Fortunately, Vassili has a beautiful wife, Liuba, who he says is like honey on the rough tongue of life. She has given him six children. Six! Gloria is the only girl.

At night, in the wooden house, the family gathers to

sing, to eat meat patties, and to drink tea from the samovar. They sit in a circle on the rug, the smaller ones between their mother's legs, the older ones around Vassili. Gloria is always to his left.

"One of these days," Vassili explains to his sons, "what I own will be yours. Not only the bounty of this land, with its miraculous fruit, but also the headaches that come with it. All of it will be yours! Good riddance! As for me, I'll finally get to rest. You won't hear me grumble anymore, and my stomach won't bother me again."

Then he turns toward Gloria. "For you it will be different. You will have a choice."

Gloria frowns. "What do you mean? What choice?" she wants to know.

"You're my only daughter," Vassili answers. "If you want this house, it will be yours. But I suspect that you will want to leave."

Gloria looks at her brothers: Fotia and Oleg, with their broad shoulders; Anatoly, who squints behind his thick glasses; Iefrem, whose hair is curlier than a lamb's; and Dobromir, with his angelic smile. She looks at Liuba, her mother, who hides her face under the thickness of her black hair. She looks at the ornamentally painted furniture in the house, the rugs, the lamps that cast luminous circles on the walls. Outside she can hear the rustle of the orchard in the night wind. Why isn't there a place for her in this paradise? she wonders.

"You're wrong, Vassili. I don't want to leave!" she says.

To prove it, every day Gloria gathers her hair under a kerchief and does the same thing as her brothers: she slips on a pair of overalls and goes to work in the orchard. She learns how to take care of the trees, to protect them from parasites, to cover them with nets to keep the birds from picking at their fruit. At harvesttime she's the first one to climb the ladders, a sack around her neck, the first one to tumble down and run to the truck to unload kilos of apples in the tipper.

She grows up. She becomes as strong as Fotia, her eldest brother, and as tough as Oleg, the second-oldest one.

At sixteen she learns to drive the trucks.

At seventeen she knows how to fix engines and to oil pistons as well as any of Vassili's other workers. In the evening, her arms dirty with grease, she sits on her father's left side, her hair undone, as beautiful as a wild plant.

"I don't want to leave," she tells him again. "Why do you say I'm different?"

Vassili pulls on his suspenders to make them snap, which means that he doesn't want to answer.

Yet one day Gloria understands that she isn't like her brothers. It's the day she meets Zemzem, at the end of the line of apricot trees, near the railroad track.

Zemzem arrives in a truck with seasonal workers hired by Vassili. There are many of them—young, poor, and dust-covered—but there's something different about Zemzem. It's hard to pinpoint—almost as if he has a sun shining above his head. Right away Gloria notices him, and she nearly falls from the ladder when he looks back at her.

At noon she doesn't mingle with the fruit pickers the way she usually does. She needs to walk and think. Besides, she isn't hungry. She takes off along the railroad tracks.

When she turns around, Zemzem is there, behind her.

"I saw you take off without bringing any water," he says. "It's not good to stay in the sun without drinking." He hands her his flask. "Here you go."

Gloria suddenly sits down on one of the railroad ties. She feels dizzy.

"You see?" Zemzem smiles. "You're exhausted!"

Gloria takes the water. Her cheeks are burning.

"I saw you working," Zemzem goes on. "Very impressive! You pick fruit faster than anyone else."

Gloria is unable to utter a single word. They say this is what happens when you fall in love. But all of a sudden the tracks shake.

"The train!" she shouts.

She pushes Zemzem off to the side, where they fall on top of each other.

When the train shoots past them, they're caught in a swirl of hot, metallic air. Gloria's heart beats in rhythm with the train, *tack-a-tack-tack, tack-a-tack-tack*. It's the most beautiful day of her life.

Every day after, they meet at noon by the tracks. They balance themselves on the rails, pretending to be tightrope walkers, and make bets on the promptness of the express train. The train is old and temperamental, but usually at lunchtime they can hear it coming.

This is how, at the end of harvesttime, after they've kissed 127 times and counting, they witness the Terrible Accident.

chapter five

WHEN Gloria reaches this point in the story, I am kneeling on the bed, out of the blanket, no longer tired.

"Don't leave anything out!" I say, pounding the mattress with my fists. "Not the wounded passengers, the ripped-open cars, the fire, or anything."

Gloria rolls her eyes and, every time, waits for me to calm down. I lie on the mattress again, under the blanket, and wait until she decides to go on.

I count up to fifty as I look at the wallpaper that's coming unglued. I pretend to be bored, and when my breathing slows, she continues.

"Zemzem heard the train first—"

I cut her short. "His hearing was very sharp, right?"

"Very sharp, Koumaïl. He came from a faraway region, from a people of hunters, and his father—"

"Was the chief of the village! I know! He could even hear the murmur of the dead."

"Absolutely. That's why Zemzem heard the creaking and

whistling of the train well before I did. He squeezed my hand hard because he understood that something unusual was happening. We started to run along the tracks, and suddenly—"

"The thunder!"

"A frightening roar, Koumaïl. Like a huge explosion, followed by an earsplitting noise that made your hair stand up on your head. Then a cloud of smoke rose. When we got to the train, all out of breath and sweating—"

"Just past the curve, right?"

"Yes, where the pear trees were growing. We saw that the engine car was on fire. The other cars had come off the rails, toppled over like dominoes. People were stuck under the wreckage, screaming. Those who had managed to escape were sitting on the ground in shock, while the fire spread to the trees."

"People were burning? You saw them?"

"No, Koumaïl, I did not see them. It was the smell that was unbearable."

"Like barbecued pork!"

"Worse than that. I can't describe the smell. Zemzem told me to go and tend to the wounded, and he ran toward my father's house to get help."

"And to get the tanker truck, more than anything else!"

Gloria nods. She knows that I never forget any detail. I could tell this story myself as if I had lived it. But I prefer to listen to it.

"I rushed to the cars at the rear and helped two men lift a piece of wood that was crushing the legs of an old man. Around us, others were calling for help, but there weren't enough of us. I was able to get two children out of the fifth car through a gap. That's when I heard a woman call for help."

"*Ossecourédémoi!*" I shout in a high-pitched voice, trying to imitate a French accent. *Helpmehelpme!*

"Exactly. '*Ossecourédémoi!*' I slipped through the gap."

I laugh, looking at Gloria. "You were as thin as a nail back then. You could squeeze through without a problem."

Gloria pinches my cheek. She makes believe she's annoyed with me, but I know she's teasing.

"It's true that I have put on weight, Monsieur Blaise. But let's forget that for now. I slipped into the car and I crawled between the torn seats to the woman. She had rolled herself into a ball in a corner. There was blood on her face and in her honey-colored hair."

From this point on I never interrupt Gloria. Each word she says is of the utmost importance.

"I came near her and discovered that she was holding a baby against her chest. She begged me with her eyes, and I understood what she expected of me."

Gloria puts her hand on my forehead. She smiles with a tenderness that breaks my heart.

"This woman had a broken back; she could no longer move. I put my arm around the baby and took him. She made me understand that she was French and told me her name: Jeanne Fortune. Then she pointed to her son and whispered, 'Blaise.' That's how I saved you. When Vassili and Zemzem came back with the tanker truck, I was standing under the pear trees. I was crying. The men began by putting out the fire, and then they took axes and chain saws to cut open the cars and move the survivors out. I waited with you. You had fallen asleep on my chest. You didn't see the men carry your mother away."

I shake under the blanket, my eyes popping out. I can see it all: my mother's ashen face, her honey-colored hair matted with blood, her body as limp as a cloth. Her eyelids are closed. She is lying in the scorched grass. Is she dead? I always wonder.

"She had only fainted, I'm sure," Gloria goes on. "Ambulances came from town. I wanted to board the one that was taking your mother away, but the doctors kept me from doing so. There were too many wounded! I had to make room for them. Zemzem came near me. I showed him the baby. He put his hand on your cheek and said that you were a miracle. You opened your eyes then. Like you understood."

Night came a long while ago. I can hear the familiar noises of the Complex—voices in the hallways, footsteps on the floor above, as well as the vocal exercises of Miss Talia, a former singer in the national opera. I can't feel totally sad when Gloria tells me about the Terrible Accident and my mother's broken back. It's as if she's telling me about something that happened long ago, sort of like a legend.

Gloria gets up and pours herself a last cup of lukewarm tea. My body is heavy on the mattress.

I yawn. "You looked for my mother everywhere with Zemzem but couldn't find her," I say. "Her name wasn't registered at any of the hospitals, right? And even if you had wanted to give me back, no one wanted to look after a baby. So you kept me."

19

Gloria sighs. I see that she's tired, but she knows that I won't leave her in peace until the end of the story.

"Everything became complicated because the war started," she goes on. "In fact, the train hadn't derailed by accident. It was sabotaged. The orchard was requisitioned by the militia 'for the war effort,' or so they said. They took the house, the trucks, and even the trees! They left us only a shed. The army drafted Zemzem and my brothers. Before they left, each of them gave me a precious gift."

I know the list of precious gifts by heart.

"Fotia gave you his radio, but he forgot the battery," I say. "Oleg gave you his stringless violin. Iefrem, his green atlas. Dobromir, his warm lambskin blanket. And Anatoly, a poetry book that you've lost."

As always, I end up with the same question. "And Zemzem? What did *he* give you?"

Gloria puts a finger over her lips and answers that it's a secret. What Zemzem gave her is so precious and so beautiful that she can't say anything about it. And as always, I am disappointed. I badger and plead, always in vain.

Gloria smiles at me. "One day, maybe, I'll tell you."

"When?"

"One day."

Defeated, I sigh and ask for the end of the story.

"After my brothers and Zemzem had gone, I went to my father and mother. I told them that I was leaving too. I was responsible for you, and I had to take you away from the soldiers and the bombs. Liuba gave me her kitchen utensils. Old Vassili gave me his samovar and said, 'You see, I knew you would be leaving. Go, my daughter, and find a place where you can live a happy life.'"

"That's why he nicknamed you Gloria Bohème," I say. "'Bohème' means that you'll always be free and can cross all borders."

"Yes, Koumaïl. And then Vassili pulled on his suspenders to make them snap. He didn't want to talk anymore."

Suddenly Gloria looks sad. She lies down under the blanket on the other mattress; I can see her stomach, which rises like a hill. She coughs and coughs and coughs—enough to tear her throat out.

I swallow to undo the knot that strangles me.

"One day you'll find Zemzem and I'll find my mother," I say, hoping to make her feel better.

The log in the stove is almost burned. Gloria gets her breath back.

"And my father?" I ask. "You didn't see him in the train car?"

"No, Koumaïl, I did not see him."

The Complex is now silent.

"Go to sleep, little miracle," Gloria whispers to me in the pitch-darkness. "Tomorrow life will be better."

chapter six

THERE are all sorts of people in the Complex, including peasants who've been driven off their farms because of land requisitions, laborers who've lost their jobs, old people who've gone soft in the head, sailors without ships, women without husbands, deserters, a meditating monk, and Miss Talia, who used to sing at the opera. There is also Abdelmalik, a tall black teenager.

Abdelmalik lives right next to Emil, in the garbage shed near the Complex. No one dumps garbage there now, but the stench is embedded in the walls. And no matter how hard Abdelmalik washes and scrubs his skin, he stinks like rancid butter and putrefied peelings.

"Sorry," he says each time he goes to someone's apartment.

At first you hold your nose; after a while you get used to it.

According to Emil, Abdelmalik is nineteen years old and escaped from jail. It's in jail that he learned to fight.

"He had to!" Emil explains to me. "In jail, if you don't fight, you're dead!"

To entertain us, Abdelmalik shows us his moves in the courtyard or on the roof of the Complex when it's not too windy. We make a circle around him, and he bounces from one foot to the other, his fists at face level. *Whoosh!* He punches the air. He bends down to skirt his imaginary adversary's counterattack and *thwack!* A kick! He turns, he twirls. His arms smash invisible jaws, his legs cut and whip. We clap our hands in rhythm. It looks like a dance.

"Uugh," Emil sighs. "It's too easy! I'd like to see a real fight with a real opponent."

"We should ask Sergei," I say.

We all agree. Sergei is the only one who would know how to fight against Abdelmalik. But we're too afraid to ask him.

On some days old Mrs. Hanska gives us lessons. She boasts that she was once headmistress of a school for young girls. We don't really know what that means, but the way she swells her chest when she says it makes her look important. According to her, this qualifies her to teach us the essentials.

No one grumbles because school is a good distraction from our chores and roughhousing in the stairs. We squeeze into Mrs. Hanska's tiny apartment: The first to arrive plop on the couch, the chairs, and the floor. The last ones to get there have to stand, their backs against the front door. It's fine in winter because we keep each other warm. But in summer Mrs. Hanska's apartment is crowded with wet foreheads and dripping temples.

Mrs. Hanska teaches us to read. She picks random

subjects for her lessons from the pages of a worn-out book and makes us repeat a lot of things that we don't understand—like proverbs; the list of the Seven Wonders of the World; the Richter scale, used to measure earthquakes; the twelve feats of Hercules; and the planets of the solar system. But she also makes us learn recipes, songs, the capitals of the world, and the names of flowers.

My knowledge is vast and varied. At almost eight, I can hardly write my name, but I can recite from one to ten the mineral hardness scale without any mistakes: talc, gypsum, calcite, fluorite, apatite, feldspar, quartz, topaz, corundum, diamond.

One day when Mrs. Hanska is teaching us a Christmas song, Miss Talia rushes into the apartment. "That's enough!" she shouts, her face all red.

She steps over those of us who are seated on the floor and plants herself in front of the group. Then she opens her mouth and lets out a continuous, single-note sound. With her right hand she suddenly makes a gesture as if she's zipping her mouth shut. Total silence follows. She smiles.

"Your turn!" she says.

Timidly we open our mouths. Thirty different sounds clash against each other. Miss Talia frowns and zips her mouth again. Silence. She scratches her chin, looking puzzled, then lets out the same single note, which she repeats over and over until we're all able to produce the same sound as her.

"Phew!" she sighs. "I can't promise you that we'll sing *La Traviata* someday, but we might be able to celebrate Christmas without bursting our eardrums."

News that Miss Talia, former singer at the national opera, is teaching music to the children spreads in the Complex. This gives other people ideas! One by one, grown-ups knock on Mrs. Hanska's door to offer their services, which is how we learn

- the different species of cows
  and the different cuts of beef from Old Max;
- the names of spices and plants and their
  medicinal properties from old Lin;
- the martyred saints and prayers
  from the meditating monk;
- sewing from Betty, Rebeka's mother;
- Arabic words from Jalal and Nasir,
  the twins who deserted;
- the rules of poker, bridge, and blackjack
  from Kouzma, the former sailor.

Before long we have school every day, and the Complex becomes, as Gloria puts it, "the university for the poor." I store all the information in my head, not caring whether I'll ever need to use it. The knowledge piles up in my brain and keeps me company.

When spring comes, we ask Abdelmalik to teach us the art of fighting. He agrees, and so we find ourselves in the courtyard bare-chested, dancing from one foot to the other. With fists raised to face level—*whoosh!*—we punch the air. We bend down to avoid the counterattack and *thwack!* A kick! Our hands smash jaws, our thin legs cut and whip; we are dancing with Abdelmalik.

All of a sudden creepy Sergei appears in the courtyard. He's holding not his razor but his old pair of boxing gloves. He comes near Abdelmalik.

"You stink!" he provokes him.

"Sorry," the other says.

"Wimp!" Sergei shouts. "What did they teach you in jail?"

Sergei puts his gloves on. He shakes a little because he drinks too much, but he's scary anyway.

"So? What did they teach you? Come on! Show me!"

Abdelmalik turns around to give us a look of apology. *Bam!* Sergei takes advantage of this and sends him a right hook to the nose! A murmur of fear and excitement ripples through our group.

Emil is the first one to react. "Defend yourself, Abdelmalik!" he shouts.

Right then Abdelmalik becomes our champion. Thirty voices chant his name and echo against the Complex's walls. Soon inquisitive faces appear at the windows. I notice Gloria's in our second-floor window. She frowns.

The fight begins.

Galvanized, Abdelmalik stretches his muscles. Our attention is riveted on his strength and his insolent youth. He dodges, he jumps, he lets blows fly in Sergei's face, and the drunk loses his balance several times, but without falling. The old man takes the blows and finds his legs again. Abdelmalik's eyebrow is split. A veil of blood comes down over his left eye.

"Watch out!" Emil shouts at him hoarsely. "Stay on your guard! Bend down! Lay into him!"

Sergei's good eye burns with hatred. He spits on the ground, and the deep rancor he's bottled up against the Armenian who nearly killed him years ago floods out now.

"I'm going to pound you to a pulp, you African scumbag," he says, boiling with rage.

Insults start to fly in the crowd.

"Straighten his nose, so he won't be as ugly!" Emil yells to our hero. "Go ahead, hit him!"

Abdelmalik pounds on Sergei, following the advice. With three well-landed blows he sends the old man down and two of his teeth fly away. A last blow and creepy Sergei collapses on the wet cobblestones, his body broken.

A silence as dense as a cloud of fog hangs over the courtyard. Abdelmalik stands up, proud and magnificent, ready to fight some more. But it's over. The drunk crawls toward the canopy. He drools, he groans in shame.

That very evening rumor spreads that Sergei is gone, that he packed his belongings and that we won't ever see him again.

Gloria shakes her head. "Good Lord, I don't like this," she says. "Not at all."

I notice that she looks at our gear on the shelf.

A few days later Emil and Baksa come to get me, and we go to the garbage shed where Abdelmalik lives. We pinch our noses because it stinks so much.

We knock on the door. No response. I turn the knob. The door opens, letting out a flow of pestilence that makes us want to throw up.

Old Max appears. "It smells like a slaughterhouse," he says. "Move away!"

We stay behind him as he enters the shed.

"It's darker in here than in a chicken's backside!" he grumbles. "Wait a second."

Old Max finds the light switch and turns it on. We see Abdelmalik's body propped up against the wall. His throat has been slit. With a razor.

chapter seven

IT'S winter again and I am eight years old. Since Abdelmalik's death everyone is scared that Sergei will come back
or denounce us to the militia. Miss Talia no longer gives us
singing lessons, and Mrs. Hanska chased us from her apartment. She says that we should stay as we are and not try to
know too much.

Old Max is still willing to tell us about the different cuts
of beef—flank, skirt, rib, loin, sirloin, round—but we're so
hungry that his words are like torture.

We go back to our games in the staircase. But I can tell
that Tasmin, Rebeka, and Faïna don't feel like playing
anymore. They would rather whisper together as they
take turns brushing their hair, and draping themselves in
pieces of material found here and there. They don't believe our stories of ships lost at sea anymore. Emil, who is
smarter than me, nudges and points toward their growing
breasts.

"Do you see?" he says in a voice I don't recognize.

I go sulking back to our small room. I lie down on my mattress and Gloria asks me what's wrong.

"I've caught a despair," I say.

"Tsk, tsk, tsk!"

Gloria comes near me and inspects me from head to toe. She pulls my toes apart, rubs my tummy, scratches and tickles me gently. I end up bursting with laughter.

"If you want my advice, Monsieur Blaise, you're not sick!" she declares. "No despair has gotten hold of you."

I catch my breath and tell her that she's wrong. Ever since Abdelmalik's death everything has changed. Without the university I feel like I have an empty stomach in place of a mind.

"That's how it is with fear," Gloria explains. "Every person for themselves. But we'll leave soon. And over there it'll be better, you'll see."

"Where is over there?"

Gloria makes a vague gesture with her hand.

I think of Vassili's large mustache and snapping suspenders, of the pear and apricot trees, of the railroad track, of Zemzem, and of Gloria Bohème's five brothers. I think of Jeanne Fortune and of the French Republic. I feel torn between several wishes and I am unable to make a choice.

The water simmers in the samovar.

"Why are we at war?" I ask.

Gloria sighs. "To understand such a complicated thing, I would have to explain about the Caucasus," she says.

"And you can't?"

"No. Nobody knows how to explain about the Caucasus."

I take my green atlas. "When is the war going to end?" I press her.

"When the people are exhausted, I guess. When there are no fighters left. But it could go on for a long time because there are many of us. Children are born every day, and they grow up to become soldiers."

"Will I be a soldier?"

Gloria bolts up. "Good Lord, surely not! This war has nothing to do with the French, you know that."

I walk around our room in circles and rub my arms to keep warm.

"Nobody knows that I'm French, right?" I think out loud. "People think that I'm Russian and that my name is Koumaïl. I don't even have my mother's honey-colored hair."

"And yet, you look like her."

"Really?"

Gloria is positive about that. When she takes a close look at me, when she pushes aside some of my darker hair, she says she sees pale highlights. Honey highlights.

She hands me a cup of tea. We've been without sugar for a few weeks now, and my stomach is like a wineskin filled with sour water.

"In fact, you look like your father, too," Gloria adds.

I shake my head. "How would you know, since you've never seen him?" I ask.

"All kids look like their father, Monsieur Blaise. It's the law of genetics," she says.

I don't know what genetics is, so I keep quiet. There are so many mysteries surrounding my past that I would rather think about the future. I daydream in front of page 16 of my atlas: Paris, Nice, Lyon, the Atlantic Ocean, and Mont Blanc.

Worried, I suddenly ask, "If I go back to France one day, you'll come with me, right?"

"I'll go with you as far as I can, Koumaïl," Gloria answers in a muffled voice.

chapter eight

THAT winter I am granted the right to leave the Complex with Gloria. Until now it was out of the question. When grown-ups have work outside, the youngest have to stay protected inside. It's the rule. But I cry so hard that Gloria finally gives in.

It's not even daybreak and hail is falling. We dress, layering our clothes on top of us to brave the cold. Emil and Baksa watch me go, feeling jealous, which makes me proud.

We cross streets where drafts whistle, and we go through some dark and muddy lots. We walk along the walls of a factory, behind which chimneys appear. I hold tight to Gloria's hand. This part of the city seems sad and oppressive. The few passersby we meet walk fast, their heads down.

Finally we reach a place with crisscrossing railroad tracks, and Gloria explains to me that we are going to take the streetcar.

When we board, she pushes me to the rear and follows

me, out of breath. Her weight hampers her; I snuggle against her reassuring roundness. We're compressed in the middle of a wet crowd; unfamiliar faces, tired and mute, shake around us in rhythm with the chaos. I think of the train I was on with my mother when it derailed.

Gloria and I get off at the end of the line, in a neighborhood totally different from ours, with large boulevards, stores, sidewalk vendors, and advertising posters on top of buildings. I look around as Gloria drags me at a quick pace toward the entrance of the largest store. I manage to read the sign: *Kopeckochka*.

"Is this where you work?" I ask.

Gloria smiles at me. "Here and there," she says.

Working at Kopeckochka means sitting in the entryway, close to the sliding door, and putting your hand out toward the customers who go in and out with their shopping bags. Hot and cold air alternate with the opening and closing of the door. I cling to Gloria and try to guess which person will stop to give us a coin. Most people go by without seeing us, as if we didn't exist. Sometimes a purse opens and someone bends down.

"Thank you," Gloria says. "God bless you."

I look at her, perplexed. Usually when Gloria talks about God, it's to swear or to say that he doesn't exist. If he did, she says, he would have brought order to the Caucasus a long time ago. So is Gloria lying? I wonder.

"Tsk, tsk, tsk! I never lie, Monsieur Blaise. I may embellish things a little from time to time, that's all." She strokes my hair. "There's nothing wrong with making up stories to make life more bearable."

The door opens and closes. People go in and out. After a

while I doze off on Gloria's knees. I don't feel the heat or the cold anymore. I just recognize Gloria's familiar scent of tea and laundry, a scent that I would recognize anywhere.

Gloria shakes me awake when the day draws to a close. I stretch and rub my eyes. I don't remember where I am. Gloria shows me the coins she collected.

"Come," she says. "It's our turn to shop."

We search between the shelves of Kopeckochka. Flour, tea, sugar, dark rice. When we're done, all the coins we earned during the day disappear into the store cash register, except for one.

"Here, Monsieur Blaise," Gloria whispers. "This one's for you."

As we leave Kopeckochka, I notice that other people are sitting in the entryway, extending their hands in the draft. I come near a man who looks like Abdelmalik. He's shivering and has a dog on a leash. I give him my coin.

Before we take the streetcar back, Gloria promises me a surprise. We drag our bags along small streets that run parallel to the boulevard. The wind freezes my fingers and splits my lips. Like wreaths of smoke, food smells escape from basement windows and excite our nostrils. I am so hungry that I feel dizzy.

Gloria points to a large metal bin that sits against a wall at the back of a Turkish restaurant.

"I'm too fat to climb, but you can take a look, Koumaïl," she says.

I put my bag on the ground and jump up to grab the edge of the bin.

"Look on top!" Gloria advises me. "Take your pick!"

I can't believe what I see in the bin! I jump down with a large piece of meat—flank steak, I think—and pastries dripping with honey, which we put in a cardboard box that we happen to find.

"They're crazy to throw all this away!" I say, my mouth watering.

Gloria winks at me. "The cook in the restaurant is a friend of mine," she tells me. "We have a deal. You don't believe I'd just let you dig through any old garbage!"

In the evening I ask Emil and Baksa to meet me in the staircase. We smear our faces with honey without saying a word. It's total bliss.

Emil sighs. "Next time ask your friend to leave you some *loukoums*," he says. "I love *loukoums*."

I promise him that I will, and for a while we dream about incredible desserts overflowing with cream and stuffed with chocolate. It's one of the best moments of my life, to be seated in the staircase, my fingers all sticky, and my friends smiling from ear to ear; a moment when we forget about the war and the worries that come with it.

That night, as I sleep like a sated bear, Gloria pulls me out of the blankets.

Her face is deathly pale. In the courtyard someone is ringing the bell like crazy.

chapter nine

THE chair! The gear! Our stuff! Quick!

The Complex shakes and echoes with strange sounds. I hear *bings* and *bongs* on the courtyard pavement. In a panic, our neighbors start throwing their belongings out the windows. People are running toward the wobbly stairs. But nobody shouts, nobody cries.

Gloria picks up the khaki canvas bag with the samovar, which sticks out, and we run toward the exit of the U, hand in hand, our hearts drumming in our chests.

It's dark. We knock into other people without recognizing anyone, just like cows entering the slaughterhouse where Old Max lost three of his fingers. I can just make out Old Max, Kouzma, Jalal, and Nasir, our lookout team. They're armed with shovels and hammers, and they protect our escape by barring the street. I can hear noise farther away, along with shouts and the thumping of boots.

"The militia is making a sweep of the area!" someone whispers.

In an instant the Complex is empty. Like a disorderly stream, we flee toward the shore of the Psezkaya River. Gloria is crushing my fingers. She moves her stout body as fast as she can, while I try to make myself light, as if I hardly exist.

I don't see Emil or Baksa or Tasmin or Rebeka.

When we reach the river, there is a bridge. Blocks of floating ice reflect the moonlight. We join other fugitives who are loaded down with boxes, wheelbarrows, old mattresses, and we go across.

"You'll see how beautiful it is on the other side," Gloria whispers to me. "We're free, Koumaïl, and the world is so big!"

I hang on to her and think that Vassili was right to call her Gloria Bohème, because no militia, no river, no amount of fear can stop someone like Gloria. In my opinion, I was very lucky she found me the day of the Terrible Accident.

After we've been walking for several hours, the dawn reveals a barren countryside. I ask Gloria whether we'll go back to the Complex. She says no.

"Not even to Kopeckochka?"

"There are better stores in other places," she assures me.

"What about your friend at the Turkish restaurant? Isn't he going to worry if we don't pick up what he leaves for us in the bin?"

"He'll just give it to someone else."

I look around me. The small valleys powdered with frost, the thick pine trees, the road that disappears in the distance. The fugitives have all dispersed. I can see only a few tired silhouettes and a family that follows a cart. I am cold and hungry, as usual.

I would like to know why the militia is after us, why we don't have the right to stay in the same place a long time. I often ask Gloria about it, but her only answer is that the world is full of mysteries, take it or leave it. The only thing that comforts me is knowing that one day I will go to France. Over there, Gloria told me, there is no war.

"Is everybody rich in France?" I ask.

Gloria's face is red under her kerchief. When she talks, a cloud comes out of her mouth.

"What do you call 'rich,' Koumaïl?" she asks.

"I don't know. Maybe people give you lots of coins when you put out your hand."

"They give bills," she says.

"Oh," I say, impressed. "OK!"

Thanks to Mrs. Hanska's lessons, I know that a bill is worth more than a coin. I know the names of foreign currencies—franc, dinar, peso, dollar, crown, ruble, cruzado, zloty, lev, forint, yen. . . . I even know that there is a country where you pay with sugar, which seems pretty strange.

"I promised Emil that I would find *loukoums* for him," I say, sniffling because of the cold.

Gloria smiles and says nothing more. After a while, when it gets so cold that it hurts your lips to talk, it helps to think about pleasant things. And if your feet hurt, you have to pretend they aren't yours. They belong to somebody else. And somebody else's feet cannot be hurting you, right?

chapter ten

OUR new refuge is called Souma-Soula. It's a vast village close to mountains made of recycled materials, like bricks, wooden boards, plastic, and galvanized iron. Everything is built haphazardly, but everyone manages to find a spot, and Gloria says that we'll be living in clover. I don't want to contradict her, but I think that the Complex was much better than Souma-Soula.

"Come on, Monsieur Blaise," Gloria makes fun of me, "don't annoy me with your French manners, and help me hammer this roof."

We become friendly with the Betov family, the one that was walking with a cart on the road. There is the father, the mother, the grandmother, and the five children. They are our new neighbors. They lend us a hammer and nails, and their son, Stambek, helps us carry what we need to build a shed. Now Gloria and I have to get busy.

I learn to mix dirt, straw, and stones to fill in the gaps between the pieces of wood. I dig and flatten, I plant and lift. Gloria is very clever with her hands, thanks to what she learned at Vassili's: she covers a window opening with plastic and puts a latch on the door so that it closes.

She explains that the roof of corrugated iron must have a pitch, otherwise the snow will accumulate on top and the whole thing will collapse.

Finally, she shows me a spot behind one of the walls, where I'm supposed to dig a hole.

"What's it for?" I ask.

"Well, it will be to do our business!" she answers with a wink.

"Oh, OK."

It gives me a funny feeling to dig our toilet. In the Complex we shared toilets with the other people on the floor, but here we'll have our own private corner. Gloria says that we're becoming bourgeois. I don't understand that word, but she laughs so hard that I laugh with her, right by the edge of our future poop hole.

Stambek is nearly fifteen. He's two heads taller than me and his shoulders are as wide as a man's. He reminds me of Abdelmalik, but he's white instead of black. He and I get along: I talk, he listens.

Mr. Betov often knocks on his son's head. Afterward he says, "Quiet!" and adds, "Listen how it echoes in there!"

I prick up my ears and Stambek does too, his eyes closed, but we don't hear anything.

Mr. Betov sighs. "It doesn't matter. What's important is to have both arms," he says, grumbling.

41

Stambek smiles and rolls up his sleeves. His arms are muscular and hairy, and he's got veins that remind me of the rivers in my atlas. He motions for me to pull up my sleeves. I make a face. My arms are like twigs.

But Mr. Betov is right. At Souma-Soula everybody uses their arms to work, even the children. That's how it is if you want to eat.

We've barely finished nailing down the roof when Gloria and I head over to the hiring station. This time we won't be holding out our hands the way we did at Kopeckochka. The hiring supervisor, whom we call Chief, points to a gigantic grayish pile that undulates over kilometers. It's a sort of bare mountain. On top of it I see clusters of people who are squatting.

"You dig through the dump," Chief explains. "I'll lend you tools, which you'll bring back to me every evening. If you lose them, or if they're stolen, you'll have to pay for them. Is that clear?"

"What are we looking for?" Gloria asks.

"This!" Chief answers, taking a small metal cylinder topped with a wire out of his pocket.

He puts it in our hands so that we can see what it looks like.

"A lightbulb cap?" Gloria says, surprised.

"Exactly! But what we're interested in is the nickel wire. You dig, find the caps, and save the wire. At the end of the day you'll be paid according to the weight of the nickel you've gathered, is that clear?"

I nod as the list of elements that Mrs. Hanska made

us repeat so often comes back to my mind by bits: neon, neptunium, nickel. . . . I'm really pleased to use my knowledge.

So Gloria and I climb the mountain with our tools that look like grapnels. Chief assigns us to a spot, which we share with the Betov family. Even the grandmother, with her bad legs, is working.

"Be careful," Mr. Betov warns us, "there's broken glass everywhere. It goes under your skin if you're not careful."

I squat near Stambek. He digs at an incredible pace, sorting the caps and the nickel wires as if he has done this all his life.

At the end of the day I feel so tired that I don't even count the coins that Chief gives me. I walk like a robot to our shed and go to sleep without eating, without even a cup of tea, my cheek on my lambskin blanket.

I dream about Gloria Bohème's five brothers. I see their faces, all dirty because of the war. I see Fotia's and Oleg's bleeding shoulders. Anatoly's broken eyeglasses. Iefrem's curly hair, stiffened by mud. And Dobromir, sitting astride a cannon, with his invincible, angelic smile.

In the middle of the night Gloria's coughing wakes me up. The dog is barking and scolding in her chest. I can't bear to hear this awful noise, so I block my ears.

chapter eleven

AFTER a few weeks on the glass mountain, I'm an expert in the recovery of nickel. My grapnel digs, my fingers grab the caps, *thwack!* I pull the wire. I make twice as much money now as I did the first days, and we can afford to buy more food at the small grocery store. I'm proud of myself, but I'm worried about Gloria. She's coughing more and more; Mr. Betov says that it's because of the dust.

"This damn dust gets in your throat, deep down!" he says. "You have to be very careful!"

"Tsk, tsk, tsk," Gloria says, panting. "It's just bronchitis, it'll pass. Don't forget that I'm as sturdy as the trees, Koumaïl!"

At work, when I squat near Stambek, I talk to him about all sorts of things. I tell him about Abdelmalik and Sergei, about Vassili and Zemzem. I explain that I promised Emil I'd bring him back some *loukoums*. I teach him the different cuts of beef and the mineral hardness scale, but

Stambek's head is like a sieve. He repeats the things I say, but they don't stick in his brain.

"It's OK," I say. "This way I can tell you the same thing every day and you won't get bored."

Stambek laughs, and we keep digging cheerfully in the sharp depths of the mountain. He's a good friend. It's too bad that I'm too tired at night to play with him. The pure and simple truth is that I miss running in the staircase with Baksa, Emil, and the others. But I guess life goes on and you have to grow up.

One day I witness an accident caused by the drunk driver of a truck. It happens when everybody lines up, right where we unload our bags of nickel to be weighed. The truck starts suddenly with its load, but instead of moving forward, it backs up. People shout, jostling each other . . . too late. A little girl is crushed under the truck's wheels.

The girl's mother throws herself on the ground and pulls at her daughter's body. She lets out such a piercing wail that my hair stands on end. The driver gets out of the truck, totally unsteady. He puts his hands over his mouth when he understands what he has done. His eyes pop out. The mother screams, and the crowd looks at the driver. He takes off running like crazy, trying to get as far away as possible from the truck and the dead girl's body.

When Chief arrives, he sees the disaster. People help the mother carry her dead daughter to her shed. Silence falls over us, except for the engine of the truck, which keeps running stupidly. Then Chief gets behind the steering wheel and drives the truck to the factory, on the other side of the glass mountain.

All night I think about what happened, while Gloria coughs her lungs out.

The next morning when I go see Chief to get my grapnel, I ask him whether the drunk driver came back.

Chief shakes his head. "If he returns to Souma-Soula, people will kill him," he says.

"I know someone who can do his job," I say. "Someone who doesn't drink alcohol. Just tea, Chief!"

"Someone who can drive trucks?" he asks distrustfully.

"Yes, Chief! She can even repair engines and oil pistons, and isn't afraid to get her arms deep in grease!"

From that day on, Gloria abandons her job on the mountain. Behind the wheel of the truck, she jerks along the road full of potholes as she makes her way between the unloading zone and the factory. She's happy and so am I. When I see her not far from the spot where I sort things with the Betov family, I stand up and wave to her. Stambek does the same, and we shout, "Hello!" Gloria honks three times and flashes her lights. All the pickers of nickel are startled, and Stambek laughs like a madman until his father slaps his head. Then we calm down and go back to work. But the most important thing is that at night Gloria doesn't cough as much.

Stambek has four sisters. The youngest one is only six years old, and the oldest is thirteen. In the middle there are the twins, Suki and Maya, the ones I like best. To tell them apart, Mrs. Betov gave me a tip: Suki has a beauty spot close to her mouth, whereas Maya's is located between her eyebrows, like a period between two sentences. I look at the twins a lot, but I can't decide which one is prettier. And when one of them happens to talk to me, I mumble and I get confused. I become a complete idiot. Exactly like Gloria when Zemzem gave her his flask of water and she couldn't say a word.

Even Stambek notices that his sisters make my heart beat faster. Every time my eyes rest on them, he puckers his lips and makes kissing sounds.

"Stop it!" I tell him. "It's disgusting!"

His face drops. "Really? It's disgusting?"

"Yes!"

But, like always, he forgets everything and does it again until my cheeks become warmer than the coal under the samovar.

At night in our shed Gloria notices me daydream.

"What makes you sigh like that, Koumaïl?" she asks.

"Nothing. It's nothing."

"Just as I thought . . . you're in love."

I grumble, and Gloria laughs as she makes pancakes.

"There's nothing wrong with being in love!" she says. "It's probably the most beautiful thing in the world. When I walked with Zemzem along the railroad tracks, I was happier than ever before. . . ."

She sighs loudly and starts daydreaming too, her gaze lost through the plastic of the window.

After a while I jump up. "Is something burning?" I cry.

"God damn it!" Gloria says, retrieving the burned pancakes.

I make a face. "They're like coal now!" I say.

"Tsk, tsk, tsk! They're well done, is all!"

I sit on the floor, on top of the tarp that we found and use as a rug. We smile at each other as we chew our burned dinner. Sometimes I have the feeling that my heart is directly linked to Gloria's.

"Even if I'm in love," I say, "I'll always love you, right?"

"Of course, Monsieur Blaise! And don't forget your real mother. You must think of her, too!"

I nod to make her happy.

But as hard as I try to imagine Jeanne Fortune's frail figure and pale face, I can't see my mother as other than tall, with dark hair and red cheeks, and a little on the heavy side.

chapter twelve

ONE spring day Stambek and I go to the hiring station, but Chief refuses to give us grapnels. He says that no one is going to work today because it's a religious holiday.

"Religion is fine and a day of rest is great, but what are we going to eat tonight?" I grumble.

Suddenly Stambek decides to bring me to a spot that he discovered when he was taking a walk. When Stambek has an idea, he can't let go of it! I decide to follow him, and this is how I discover the lake.

It's about an hour away on foot from the corrugated-iron area, in a wild spot where the wind whirls. Stambek explains that he found this place when he followed a group of people carrying fishing rods. I see that there are a lot of fishermen along the shores of the lake.

"Tonight we'll eat fish!" my friend shouts.

We don't have fishing rods, but we're handy, and given the diverse rubbish that's around us, we're not short of supplies. An old radio antenna, a plastic thread, a rusty nail—and we're ready.

We make our way over the soft bank, our shoes sinking in the mud. On the opposite shore I see partially collapsed concrete buildings. According to Stambek, that's all that is left of the lightbulb factory. I try to imagine a time when the thousands of lightbulbs were new, unbroken, their nickel wires incandescent, but it's a waste of time. That era is gone, just like Vassili's orchard, just like my life as a baby in my mother's arms, or like the peace in the Caucasus.

I look for worms in the mud, and Stambek hooks them on the nail. We look at them as they squirm and we cast our fishing line. Then we wait in silence, motionless, for fish to bite.

Fishing is a little like holding out your hand at Kopeck-ochka: it takes a long time to get anything, and even then it's often disappointing. If the wind weren't so strong, I'd fall asleep.

After a while, though, the line moves and suddenly tightens. We jump up. Stambek begins pulling with all his strength.

"A big one! A big one!" he shouts as a silvery back and fin float up. "Hurry, Koumaïl!"

I rush to help. I lean over to catch the line, when suddenly I slide on the slippery bank and fall into the ice-cold lake. I sink! I choke on a mouthful of water! *Helpmehelpme!*

Stambek lets go of everything and pulls me out. I'm shaking all over, my lips are blue, and my ears are sore. The big fish is gone, together with the radio antenna, the line, and the nail.

I'm the only thing that Stambeck has caught.

I cough up putrid water from my lungs, then I throw up, and Stambek takes me back home straightaway.

Back in the shed my teeth are chattering so much that Gloria says she thinks she hears Spanish castanets. She swears as she undresses me. My clothes are so stiff with cold that they're like cardboard.

"God damn it, Koumaïl!" she groans. "What a strange idea to go swimming in this kind of weather."

She rubs me hard enough to skin me, but I keep shivering and I can't say a word. My thoughts are frozen in my head.

Stambek and Mr. Betov come back, their arms loaded with blankets. They take me to the corner of the room where Gloria has set up a stove, and they cover me with several layers and start a fire. Stambek mumbles some excuses as his father slaps his head.

"There's nothing in there!" he keeps repeating. "Nothing but wind!"

I fall into such a deep sleep that it feels as if I'm sinking to the center of the earth.

chapter thirteen

I'M sick. I can't get up. I can't do anything.

Gloria can't stop working, otherwise we won't have any money. So Mr. Betov asks his daughters Suki and Maya to take turns watching me while Gloria drives the truck.

"We are a large family and yours is small," Mr. Betov says. "I can lend my daughters for a few days!"

My illness lasts exactly six days.

The twins stay by my bedside. They burn fragrant herbs; they dab my feverish forehead with a wet cloth and put their cool hands under my neck to help me sit up. They make me drink tea. Liters of it! With honey and extracts.

I try to remember the names of the medicinal plants old Lin taught us at the university for the poor. In the fog of my fever, I recite: "Suma powder, excellent tonic . . . *Eucalyptus globulus* to treat sinus infections . . . cinnamon oil to soothe a cough and fever . . . camphor for massages . . ."

Suki takes my pulse. Her fingers are as light and delicate

as a bird's legs. I tell her silly things, and when she laughs, I see her beauty spot disappear in a dimple.

Maya sings. Her voice lulls me and I go to sleep without coughing, submerged by a flow of sweetness. When I wake up, I feel her face near me, with the beauty spot that punctuates the sentence of her eyebrows. I ask her what is written there.

She squints a little and answers.

"Suki is right! You just say any foolish thing, Koumaïl!"

Unlike Stambek, Maya and Suki don't have wind in their heads. They tell me what their life was like before the war, when they lived in a large brick house, far from Souma-Soula. One day a bomb fell and their house collapsed. Stambek stayed for three days and nights under the debris, and everybody thought he was dead.

"But when the rescuers got him out, he was whole!" Maya smiles. "It took us a while to notice that his mind had stayed in the rubble."

Suki sighs. "Maybe one day we'll find it again," she says. "The war has taken many things from many people."

I shiver under my blankets. "But if your house hadn't collapsed," I say, "if the train hadn't derailed, if the militia hadn't taken Vassili's orchard, and if they hadn't chased us to the other side of the Psezkaya River, I wouldn't have fallen in the lake."

"So?" Suki inquires, perplexed.

I turn red and shut my eyes. War is bad, that much is true. And it's true that it has taken many things from many people. But it has also given me Gloria and my first taste of love. How can you explain something so strange? I wonder.

When Gloria comes back from work, her face so coated in road dust that she looks like a relative of Abdelmalik, I ask her if one has the right to be happy in wartime. She looks at me gravely and wipes her dirty cheeks before answering.

"To be happy is recommended at all times, Monsieur Blaise!" she says.

chapter fourteen

UNFORTUNATELY, the best of times have to come
to an end. I have no choice but to get better and go back to
work on the mountain. From now on I am forbidden to ac-
company Stambek on his walks, and he's not allowed to go
to the lake anymore. But Suki and Maya still visit us in the
evening.

We are less tired now that we're used to working hard.
We sit on the tarp and play with cards that I made out of
cardboard. I teach them the rules of poker, bridge, and
blackjack the way Kouzma taught us, which means cheat-
ing. Suki has lots of fun, and Maya gets irritated because she
doesn't like to lose. When we need a fourth player, we call
Stambek.

"It's very simple," I say. "You have five cards. When two
of them have the same numerical rank, you've got a pair. If
you have three of the same numerical rank, it's even better.
If all your cards are of the same color, it's a flush."

Stambek concentrates so hard that he breaks into a

sweat. It's sad to see him like this, with his brain full of holes! I promise myself that one day I'll take my grapnel and, instead of looking for nickel wires, I'll dig in the ruins to recover Stambek's intelligence.

"Well, I'm sleepy," Maya says suddenly.

"Yes, I'm exhausted," Suki adds.

We put the cards aside, and Stambek is relieved to be going back home. Before they leave, the twins kiss me on the cheek. My heart lights on fire faster than dry straw. But as soon as they're gone, the fire dies down and a feeling of emptiness fills my stomach. Love makes me feel hot and cold; the pure and simple truth is that I'm not sure I can survive it.

More and more wounded soldiers arrive in Souma-Soula. Some have lost an eye, a leg, an arm. Some have lost their minds and wander around shouting like crazy. That's all we see of the war. Mr. Betov says that "the theater of operations" is far from us, somewhere up north, and that we are refugees. I like the word "refugees." It must mean that we are sheltered, which reassures me.

In my mind, war looks like a ferocious and famished beast hiding in the nooks of the mountains and the dark forests shown on page 79 of my green atlas. I put my finger on the winding roads and imagine the unavoidable advance of armies looking for one another. Bombs crush and rip villages open. War chases families away, destroys pasturelands, gobbles up soldiers. It is voracious.

Sometimes I think about Zemzem and about Gloria's brothers. This monstrous animal may have devoured them.

I don't dare ask Gloria what she thinks, because I don't want to make her sad.

"And what if the war comes to Souma-Soula?" is the only thing I say. "What will we do?"

"What we've always done, Koumaïl," she answers. "Walk straight ahead toward new horizons."

"OK, but we'll go with the Betovs, right?"

"Who knows? There are so many ways to get lost. Especially in the Caucasus!"

I study the maps again and I see the dotted lines of borders that get entangled from one valley to the other. I see Georgia, Abkhazia, Armenia, Chechnya, North Ossetia and South Ossetia, Ingushetia, Dagestan. . . .

Gloria shakes her head. "Too many countries," she says. "Too many people! Borderlines move and names change constantly. At the end of the day, only ruins and unhappy people are left. It's useless to try to understand the Caucasus, Monsieur Blaise. Leave it alone. It's not your concern, little French guy, OK?"

"OK."

I turn the pages. My fingers slide west, following winding paths, until I land in France, as usual. No war. No militia. Things are much simpler over there, thanks to the republic.

"What would be nice," I say, "is for all of us to go there. Even Vassili, Zemzem, your brothers, Emil and Baksa. And my father, too, if we can find him. That would be a good surprise for my mother. We could organize a big reunion!"

I get overexcited: we could even go farther, per page 17, up to England! Gloria bends over my shoulder to study the route with me. We jump over the mountains, the dotted lines, the rivers, and my finger reaches France, where there is a town named Calais.

"We'll take a boat because there's no bridge," I say.

"No need. Even better, there's a tunnel," Gloria explains to me. "Engineers spent a lot of time studying the best way to dig it. It was finished last year."

"A tunnel under the sea?"

"Exactly!" Gloria says. "A tunnel with a train."

I can hardly believe this. My finger stays on this part of the world where people were digging under the sea. "I want to cross the English Channel through the tunnel," I say. "The two of us."

"OK," she says.

Gloria never discourages my dreams. But she tells me that in the meantime I have to go to sleep because it's late. I ask her to tell me my story, with every detail, like always. As I lie half-asleep, the trains get jumbled and I see the express train catch on fire as it cuts through waves and shoves aside bewildered fish.

chapter fifteen

WINTER returns to Souma-Soula, and a rumor circulates from shed to shed that a curse has fallen over the dwellers of the lake area. It seems that several women have given birth to monstrous children.

"The first one didn't have a head!" Suki tells me.

"The second one had two of them!" Maya says with a grimace.

"Who told you that?" I ask.

"Chief! He saw them!" they both say.

After further investigation it turns out that Chief didn't see anything, but that he knows an older Russian man whose sister-in-law gave birth to a child with three arms.

"Ugh!" the girls cry out. "Three arms!"

The grown-ups refuse to believe us until Gloria meets a special convoy on the road to the factory.

"Men in armored cars," she tells me. "They were wearing coveralls, glasses, and masks over their mouths."

"Like astronauts?"

"Exactly! And they were going straight to the lake. It must be serious!"

Shortly after that we learn that fishing is forbidden and that all access to the lake has been cordoned off. The men in coveralls have set up tents. According to Mr. Betov, they are scientists sent by the government to analyze the water, the soil, and even the innards of the fish. It seems likely that the lake has been spoiled by toxic waste coming from the former lightbulb factory. This would explain the birth of monstrous children. But how, exactly? Nobody knows! Everyone is fearful. Several families have already left the area, and others are beginning to pack up.

As a result, Mr. Betov gives me sideways glances, as if I were headless or had a third arm growing out of my back. Suddenly I feel ill at ease.

"Sorry, Koumaïl, but you fell in the lake's poisoned water," he tells me. "One has to be careful. As long as we don't know what's going on, Suki and Maya can't visit you anymore. And I have to ask you to work at a distance from us. I hope you understand?"

His words strike me like a blow. To be kept away is the worst thing that has ever happened to me. I cry a long time in Gloria's arms, shouting that it's unfair, that I'm not sick, and that if I hadn't fallen in the lake, we would have eaten fish and would all be contaminated.

But it's too late.

Suki and Maya avoid me. They keep their heads down and walk faster when they see me. As for Stambek, he looks very sad but he obeys his father.

* * *

I no longer have a sense of belonging on the mountain of glass. I'm like a wounded soul, alone with my grapnel and my sorrow. To cheer myself up, I dig through the trash and look for strings for Oleg's violin and batteries for Fotia's radio. I manage to find what I need; now instead of playing cards at night, I fix the precious things. When I'm done, the violin squeaks a sinister sound and the radio crackles.

"Better than nothing!" Gloria says encouragingly.

But I can see that she's forcing herself to smile.

More and more families are leaving, and army recruiters fall on us like locusts on the harvest. They come to recruit volunteers for the front. One day I see Chief in a military truck with other men. He makes a V sign to me as they take off, and I remain alone in the gusts of autumn wind.

I wander the streets, which feel chilled with an atmosphere of doom, as Gloria struggles to keep driving the now half-filled truck. She will drive as long as possible because each coin earned is a step toward the future.

"What future?" I ask with a sigh.

"Come on, Koumaïl, cheer up! You're much too young to say such things!"

But one morning I discover that the Betovs' shed is empty. Nothing left. No pots or pans, no blanket. They left without even saying goodbye.

I stand in the deserted room, my throat so knotted that I cannot breathe.

When I turn around, I see one of my playing cards pinned on the door. I remove it. It's the ace of hearts: the only message of love that Suki and Maya had time to leave me.

chapter sixteen

I am ten now, with a broken heart and bleeding feet and an empty stomach. And once again I'm walking on endless roads toward the unknown with Gloria and our gear. We're refugees without refuge, and I really believe that I've caught a despair.

"Tsk, tsk, tsk!" Gloria says. "If I give you a thorough inspection, Koumaïl, I'm sure that I won't find any parasites!"

I shrug. "Don't bother. I'm older. I know that what I feel has nothing to do with lice."

Abruptly Gloria stops walking and gives me a sideways glance. She throws the gear on the ground and opens it. We are in the middle of a snow-covered field, under a heavy sky filled with circling crows. What is she doing? I wonder. Does she think I want to camp here?

"It's true that you've grown a lot, Koumaïl," she says as she looks into the opening of the gear. "It's time that I confide in you what my secret remedy is."

I sigh. The snow is drenching my pants up to the knees

and I ache all over. We've walked for at least a million kilometers. The scientists at Souma-Soula ordered us to evacuate from what they classified as a "dangerous zone." What can Gloria possibly find to make me feel better? I want to know. Is she going to pull Suki, Maya, and Stambek out of her bag like a magician?

"Ah, here we are!" Gloria smiles as she shows me her old tin box.

She removes her gloves, and for the first time she opens the box in front of me. In spite of my bad mood, curiosity makes me come closer.

"I knew that one day we would need this," Gloria says. "And that day has come."

At first I see nothing but a pile of papers. Then Gloria unfolds them, and I stare wide-eyed when I understand what they are: a fat wad of bank notes—of American dollars. And, rolled inside them, two small notebooks with the universal word "passport." Inside the passports are lines written in an alphabet I can't read.

"This passport is in your name: Blaise Fortune," Gloria explains. "The other one is your mother's passport: Jeanne Fortune. The pictures are missing, but we'll get new ones before we board."

"Board? But . . ."

I've grown up, it's true, but I'm not sure that I understand. Gloria laughs when she sees the puzzled expression on my face.

"The one and only remedy against despair, Koumaïl, is hope! That's what I have in my box: hope!"

She puts the lid back on, satisfied.

"We're going to use the passports?" I ask in disbelief.

"Exactly!"

"But . . . you're going to take my mother's place, then?"

"Yes." Gloria smiles. "And at last you will officially be Monsieur Blaise."

I can't believe my ears. Around us there is only snow, sky, and crows, a kind of hazy landscape without limits, where dollars and passports are of no use.

"Where are we going?" I ask.

"To France!" Gloria answers cheerfully as she lifts the gear over her back. "So, are you coming?"

chapter seventeen

THE next million kilometers seem much easier to me. Knowing we have a destination is like having wings! Snowfields, gravel fields, bare forests where invisible owls hoot— it makes no difference. I walk relentlessly. And relentlessly I pester Gloria with questions: France, but where exactly? I want to know. There are so many towns! And what boat will we board? What is its name? Once we get to where we're going, what will we do? And how is it that she has my mother's passport?

Gloria explains that Jeanne gave it to her, together with mine, when she was in the train wreck, before she lost consciousness.

"You never told me that!" I protest.

"Well, now you know."

"And the photos?"

"I was afraid. I burned them."

I frown. "And the money?"

"Zemzem gave me the box. He wanted to give us a

chance to get away, to cross borders and controls. Being called Bohème is not enough to leave a country at war."

"So that was his gift? A box and dollars?"

"Only part of the gift," Gloria confesses. "I might tell you the rest . . . but later."

I am both troubled and vexed that Gloria never mentioned these passports to me. What if she hasn't been telling me the simple truth about the Terrible Accident and about my mother? I start to think. Yet I have no choice but to trust her.

We trek across villages with muddy streets and telephone poles whose torn cables swing in the wind like people hanged; we trek across flooded fields; we trek along roads that go nowhere and vast countryside where nothing grows.

The people we encounter have emaciated dogs and hostile faces. They lock their doors when they see us. Do they know that we come from Souma-Soula's "dangerous zone"? I wonder. Is it written on our faces?

"Don't pay attention to them," Gloria advises me. "Move on as if you were a ghost."

I do my best to imagine that I am nothing, just a draft of air. . . . But days go by like this and I begin to feel sadness weigh heavily again on my chest, worse than if I had swallowed a grapnel.

From time to time, having no strength left, we have to steal something to eat—some warm bread on a windowsill, some dry meat, or some pickles in vinegar.

Along the way we come across trucks covered with tarps

that move more slowly than a hearse and are headed north with their loads of ashen-faced soldiers. No one makes the V sign.

At night we sleep in barns, in churches, even in hen-houses. In the morning we stink of droppings and rotten straw.

"Courage," Gloria keeps repeating. "We'll be there soon."

But I don't see any port. Never mind a boat on which to embark. France is a faraway and out-of-reach dream, more so now that we don't have any coal to boil water in the samovar.

Gloria takes my hand. "Soon we'll leave the mountains, Koumaïl," she tells me. "In the valley you'll see a river. At the end of the river, there is an estuary that opens onto a large sea and a city that opens onto a port. The air will be sweet and you'll see palm trees, Koumaïl. Over there we'll find people to help us. I'll manage, I promise."

I move on, trying to imagine this improbable city from where we will board a boat to go to other, just as improbable cities. But something nags at me.

"At the border they'll see that you're not French," I say.

"Tsk, tsk, tsk! And why would they?"

"You can't even speak French."

"So what? You can't either, Monsieur Blaise! Yet you're French, aren't you?"

When I make a list of my French vocabulary, I know only a few words in the language of my country of origin: *"Helpmehelpmeplease."* Gloria's argument leaves me speech-less. So I keep on walking and try to believe that my feet are somebody else's.

We finally reach the river, then the estuary and the port of Sukhumi. Beyond the palm trees, cargo vessels and military ships adorned with cannons lie hull after hull.

Night falls over buildings in ruin. It rains. The docks are littered with debris but also with men, women, and children who have nowhere to go and who sleep here and there, taking shelter under tarps. I am so tired that I am ready to sleep under the rain with the dogs and the garbage.

"Tsk, tsk, tsk," Gloria tells me. "There is better for us tonight! Come on."

She drags me through backyards and smelly streets up to the entrance of a bar, the Matachine.

The room is dark, with wobbly tables and cigar-smoking men who stare at us. Gloria pushes me toward a bench and asks me to wait for her.

As Gloria heads toward the bar, I make myself cozy and put my head down against the sticky armrest. I can't hear what she says to the man who is opening the beer bottles. They talk a long time, while I fall into a deep sleep.

When Gloria wakes me up, she smiles broadly.

"Everything is arranged," she tells me. "We'll board a boat in a few days. For the time being, we're going to settle in upstairs."

Her finger points to the ceiling of the Matachine.

We climb a stiff ladder up to a narrow trapdoor, and Gloria breathes with difficulty because of her weight. Finally we put our gear in a sort of cupboard in the attic: our new refuge.

The place is dusty, cluttered with boxes, but it has a dormer window. Gloria unfolds two camping beds right under it. This way, she tells me, we will see the stars and it will be wonderful.

I lie down. I look up. The sky is pitch-black.

"Be patient," Gloria murmurs. "There are stars behind the clouds, always. Don't fall asleep, Koumaïl, watch the sky."

Drops of rain crash onto the glass, and Gloria coughs a little. I wrap myself in Dobromir's blanket, sheltered, struggling to keep my eyes open. I try to remember the names of the stars that Mrs. Hanska chose from her old book: Betelgeuse, Aldebaran, Merak, Vega. . . .

Suddenly, thousands of sparkles illuminate the sky.

"There they are!" I say.

But Gloria doesn't answer me. She's fast asleep.

The points of light disappear, and I hear the humming of engines and then muffled noises that shake the walls of the Matachine.

Those are not stars.

I hide my head under the blanket and close my eyes. Far away a bomb explodes in the port of Sukhumi.

chapter eighteen

IT'S early in the day still and I don't know where we are going. Gloria drags me along demolished streets, where there are mangy dogs and people pulling carts. She explains to me that Sukhumi was a nice town before the war, a seaside resort where people came on vacation to soak up the sun and enjoy the beaches. In summer, under the palms trees and the flowering tangerine trees, people used to eat ice cream, barefoot in sandals. It's the pure and simple truth. Now Sukhumi is an ugly place, and if people walk barefoot, it's because they've lost their shoes under the ruins of what was once their home. Only a few vestiges of the past glory days remain: big, empty hotels; waterless fountains; rusty pontoons on the shore; and collapsed walls. Still, I try to imagine how magnificent it must have been here, before the bombs, before the soldiers and the fear. I'd like to understand why those days are gone, but I know that it's a waste of time. Gloria will only tell me again to leave the Caucasus where it is, that it's not the concern of a French boy. That we have to hurry along.

"Why don't you tell me where we're going? Is it a surprise?" I ask her.

She doesn't answer, so I grow suspicious.

"Good or bad?" I ask.

Gloria pulls on my hand. I jump over the deep, rain-filled potholes of the avenues.

Finally we arrive in front of a large building. There are letters, partly erased, above the door. I read: PU_LI_ BA__

"Puliba?" I say.

Gloria winks at me. "Come on."

We go through the front door and enter an echoing hall. Several women with children are in line in front of a counter managed by a heavy lady with tired eyes. We give her a few coins before taking a flight of stairs that goes underground.

"I knew we would be lucky," Gloria tells me. "The water has not been cut off yet."

Once we're downstairs, warm steam and the scent of perfumed soap suffocate me. Finally I understand that, including the missing letters, "puliba" means "Public Baths."

Gloria removes her shoes and then all her clothes. I'm startled by how plump she is. I stand on the tiled floor, frozen like a statue.

"Come on, Koumaïl, don't be a baby!" Gloria laughs. "You've faced more difficult situations before!"

I think about what I've lived through since the Terrible Accident, and I know she's right. A moment later, as bare as worms, we disappear into the deliciously warm cloud of the hammam.

* * *

81

I let go of my tiredness, my fear, even some of my sadness, and let them run down the drain with the water of the showers; I feel much lighter. When we come out, we're as red as newborn babies.

Gloria's cheeks probably look as appetizing and shiny as the apples in Vassili's orchard. She combs my hair, buttons my shirt, and looks at me with satisfaction.

"You're as clean as a new coin!" she says. "I'm sure that you'll please Mr. Ha."

I've never heard of Mr. Ha. "Is this another surprise?" I want to know. "And why do I need to please him?"

"Stop asking questions and follow me," Gloria says. "We have something very important to take care of before curfew."

I hang on to her hand, and we make our way along the streets in the opposite direction.

Mr. Ha is a Chinese man. He's waiting for us at the back of a hash house, where other Chinese people are eating spicy soup in silence. My mouth starts to salivate, but we haven't come here to fill our stomachs.

Mr. Ha takes us to a room barely larger than a cupboard and closed off by a curtain. Gloria takes a wad of dollars out of her pocket, along with our passports.

Mr. Ha looks at them. He smiles.

"Ah, yes, France!" he says. "What a beautiful country!"

He pockets the dollars and then directs me to a stool. I wince. Is he going to shave my hair like creepy Sergei? I wonder.

"Come on," Gloria encourages me. "You have nothing to fear."

I sit down cautiously. Mr. Ha rummages behind the curtain and then brings out a gleaming camera that stands on a tripod. He positions it in front of me. I turn toward Gloria. I get it! I'm getting a new picture for my passport! That's why we went to the puliba first! A French kid can't be dirty.

"Look this way," Mr. Ha orders me. "That's good. Now keep your eyes on the lens and think about the Eiffel Tower."

I frown. "What *eiffeltower?*" I say.

"Come on, young man, everyone knows the Eiffel Tower!"

I shake my head. All I know are the pages in my atlas with the names of towns, rivers, mountains—I can even tell you the distance in kilometers between Paris and Marseille—but I have never seen a tower with the name Eiffel.

Mr. Ha sighs and heads behind his curtain. He comes back with a sort of catalog. There's a picture on each page—a picture that represents one of France's monuments.

"There!" he says, showing me. "That's the Eiffel Tower. Take a good look."

I stare at the image of a big iron edifice in the shape of an arrow planted in the blue sky. The caption, in Russian, says, "The Eiffel Tower, the Champ de Mars, the Seine, the Iéna Bridge, the riverboats."

"So, young man? Are you ready?"

I look up at the lens. I think very hard about this

pointed tower, the bridge arched over the Seine, and I imagine that I'm on it. *Click!*

"Perfect! A true little Parisian!" Mr. Ha laughs. "All right, now. Off you go!"

As Gloria sits on the stool to be photographed, I flip through the catalog. That's how I discover Montmartre and its artists, the crowded Champs-Elysées, the Palace of Versailles, Chartres Cathedral, the Bridge of the Gard, and also Mont-Saint-Michel, which is surrounded by the sea.

Mr. Ha leans over my shoulder. He looks with me at the sea, the sand, and the golden angel at the top of the mount.

"You can have the booklet, if you want it," he tells me. "Learn everything, my boy, you'll need it."

He suggests that we come back in two days, and we leave the hash house followed by the stares of the soup eaters.

Outside it's almost twilight. It will be curfew soon; it's time to go back to our refuge. With Mr. Ha's catalog under my arm, I ask Gloria what we'll do when we have our passports.

"We'll be able to go wherever we want," Gloria answers. "Jeanne and Blaise Fortune will be free citizens."

I think about this, puzzled. Although I know that my real name is Blaise, I feel sad at the idea of abandoning Koumaïl. The day we board the boat, I know a part of me will stay in Sukhumi like a piece of luggage abandoned on the dock. A suitcase filled with memories and regrets.

Suddenly I have an idea, and I pull on Gloria's sleeve.

"If you become Jeanne, I'll have to call you Mother for real," I say.

Gloria looks at me so seriously that it cuts my breath short.

"Do you think you can do that?" she wants to know.

I think about it; then I nod and repeat what she told me the day we were sitting at the entryway of Kopeckochka.

"There's nothing wrong with making up stories to make life more bearable," I tell her.

chapter nineteen

THE night bombings intensify. Everyone says that the har-
bor is destroyed, and Mr. Ha sighs loudly when he hands us
our passports. They look good, but he tells us that it's impossible to board any boat now. Too dangerous! We have to wait!

"Be patient," Gloria says when she notices my disap-
pointment. "These are the hazards of life. We have to take
them in stride."

So we stay cooped up in the attic of the Matachine,
watching the planes through the dormer window and hoping for a truce.

I'm not bored because I have my catalog of France to
study. I pester Gloria with facts about the Romans, Vercinge-
torix, and Charlemagne. The catalog is in Russian, of
course, except for the last pages, where there is some everyday French vocabulary in phonetics.

"Repeat after me," I say. "*Mercijevouzenpri.*" *Thankyou-
verymuch.*

"*Mercijevouzenpri.*"

"Not bad. *Uncafésilvouplé.*" *Acoffeeplease.*

"*Uncafésilvouplé.*"

"Good. *Pardonmeussieujevoudrèalléalatouréfel.*" *Pardonsiridliketogototheeiffeltower.*

"*Pardonmeussieuje* . . . You're tiring me out, Koumaïl. It's too difficult!"

"OK, I'll learn by myself. But don't complain if you get lost in the streets of Montmartre."

Gloria often goes down to the bar to talk with the man who opens the beer bottles. I'm not allowed to go with her because it's none of my business. When she comes back up, she brings food with her. Then she presses her ear against Fotia's radio and stays like that for hours, totally absorbed. She says she listens to the war news, but I think that all she hears are crackling sounds.

Then one evening the trapdoor opens and two heads appear above the floor.

"This is Nour and Fatima," says the man who opens the beer bottles. "Squeeze up a bit, there's no other way in."

He unfolds two other camping beds, and Gloria puts coal in the samovar while I stare at Fatima.

She sits on the bed and undoes the scarf that covers her hair. I have never seen anyone so beautiful. For the second time in my life, I fall in love. That, too, I can't help. These are the hazards of life, right?

Fatima is seventeen. She doesn't look like Suki or Maya. Fatima is unique.

Her face is golden, her lips are very thin, and her voice

fills me with sadness when she sings—which she does a lot of! She talks to me about her old life, when she went to the school in her town. Her favorite subjects were math and geometry. With her hands she draws figures—cones, triangles, diamonds. . . . It looks like a dance. I tell her about what I learned in our university for the poor, and Fatima praises me.

"You know so many things for your age, Koumaïl!" she says. "I'm sure that you'll become someone very important!"

I turn red, but Fatima can't see me because she keeps her eyes closed. She's been like this since the militia killed her father somewhere to the east of the Caucasus.

Nour, her mother, tells us what happened:

"They came into our house with Kalashnikovs. They shot my husband. Fatima saw him fall on his prayer rug. Ever since, she refuses to open her eyes."

Nour cries a lot, and Gloria pulls her to her bosom. She whispers words meant for adults—words about ethnic minorities, genocide, international tribunal—but it's obvious that Nour has caught a despair.

Seated on my bed, I wonder what color Fatima's eyes are. I'd also like to know what she sees behind the curtain of her eyelids. Is it the clear rectangle of light coming through the dormer window? I wonder. Images of her past? Her father's blood? Just darkness? I don't dare ask her any questions. We all live with our ghosts, and I know you can't disturb them too much, otherwise the sorrow that lies in our chests will wake up. It's better to concentrate on the present, on our refuge, with the boiling tea of the samovar and the desire to move toward other horizons.

"What are you reading?" Fatima asks me.

"How do you know I'm reading?"

"I hear the rustle of pages, silly. My ears aren't clogged."

I tell her about Mr. Ha and the catalog. I describe the Eiffel Tower, Notre Dame, and the Mediterranean coast, which looks just like Sukhumi before the war. Fatima smiles.

"You're lucky to be going there," she says. "My mother and I are going to Saudi Arabia."

I consult my atlas. Saudi Arabia appears on page 80, south of the Caucasus. According to my map, it's an immense desert of sand. I tell Fatima she should come with us instead, but she shakes her head. It's simpler for her to go to Saudi Arabia because she has an aunt who works there, and because of the Muslim religion.

"France is not a Muslim country," she explains to me. "It's a Christian country."

I am so disappointed about this religion issue that I go find Gloria.

"Is France a Christian country?" I ask her.

"France doesn't have a religion, Koumaïl."

"Oh? But are there Muslims in France?"

She says yes, there are some. In France you can believe whatever you want, say whatever you want, and do whatever you want because it is a country that believes in human rights.

"So if Fatima comes to France, will she be able to pray to Allah on her rug?" I want to know. "Will anybody bother her if she hides her hair under a scarf? Will anybody shoot at her with a Kalashnikov?"

"France stands for liberty, equality, fraternity," Gloria

says with assurance. "No one there is going to pass judgment on his or her neighbors because of a rug or because of their hair. It's not worth it, OK?"

"OK!"

I hurry to repeat this to Fatima. I want to convince her to come with us. But she stubbornly shakes her head.

"We must each follow our destiny," she says. "And, Allah willing, may peace come back to the Caucasus so that everyone can return home. Maybe then we'll see each other again, Koumaïl."

"But that might take a long time," I say, getting upset. "And what if it never happens? Why do we have to wait for Allah's will?"

Two small tears slide from under Fatima's closed eyelids. There is no answer to such a question.

I touch her hand and we lie down on our camping beds, side by side, as timid stars shine through the dormer window.

"If Allah is willing, you'll open your eyes," I say, dreaming out loud. "Peace will be here. You'll see people walk barefoot under Sukhumi's palm trees. And I'll be grown up and as strong and as muscular as Stambek. And then I'll ask you to marry me. And I'll take you wherever you want to go, to Vassili's orchard or to Mont-Saint-Michel. And everybody will be there—Zemzem and Gloria, her five brothers, Emil and Baksa . . . everybody."

I say all the things that go through my head—all stupid kid things. But Fatima doesn't make fun of me. She holds my hand tightly in hers and she sings. She knows better than to shatter my dreams; I'll just lose another piece of my heart. Then only crumbs of it will be left.

chapter twenty

AMONG the precious things in our gear, the one Fatima likes best is Oleg's violin. I put it on her knees with the bow. She runs her fingers along the curves of the body, the scroll, and then plucks the strings.

"Hmmm. Funny sound!" she says.

"The strings were gone, so I repaired it myself with wires I found in a dump," I tell her.

Fatima takes the bow, secures the instrument under her chin, and starts playing. At first the tune is timid, but soon the notes get louder, until they soar, and answer each other. It's a miracle that leaves me speechless.

When she finishes, her face is radiant. "It doesn't sound like much, but it's beautiful anyway," she says. "My father taught me music. Do you want to try?"

She hands me the violin and sits next to me. Gropingly she guides my hands. Her hair grazes me. I feel her breath on the nape of my neck.

"Are you scared?" she asks.

"No."

"So why are you shaking, silly?"

I try to contain my violent heartbeats. I concentrate, but Oleg's violin resists, and Fatima laughs as she listens to my awful *squeak-squeak*. Never mind! I would take all the music lessons in the world to feel Fatima's breath on my skin. . . . "Show me again! Teach me! Help me!" I tell her.

The only problem is that I'm grating on everybody's ears and nerves. After a while Gloria begs me to stop.

"You don't like music, is that it?" I say, vexed.

"Of course I do, Koumaïl. That's precisely the point!"

Laughing, Fatima puts the violin back in its box. She promises that we'll try again when Nour and Gloria go down to settle their business at the bar, something that happens at least once a day.

In fact, it's the time I like best—being alone with Fatima. I read my catalog to her with the everyday French expressions, like "*Oupuijetrouvéunbonrestaurant?*" *Wherecanifindagoodrestaurant?* Or "*Jesuimaladéjevoudrèvoirunmédecin.*" *Imsickandineedadoctor.* Fatima repeats them, twisting her mouth in all directions. We also have a game: listening to the street noises. Fatima tells me what she hears, and I lean through the open dormer window to tell her what I see—a bicycle braking, two men insulting each other, a car accident, cats fighting. . . . She can guess a lot of things, and I think that her sense of hearing is as good as Zemzem's.

"Do you know what Zemzem means in Arabic?" she asks me. "It means 'murmur of water.'"

"Really?"

"And do you know what your name means, Koumaïl?"

"No."

"It means 'universal.'"

I don't want to confess that Koumaïl is not my real name. That I'm really a French boy lost in the Caucasus.

Nour and Gloria finally come back up to the attic with corn pancakes, rice, and even meatballs with onions. We divide the feast into four equal parts, seated on the floor around the samovar.

Everything is fine up until the day when Fatima and I hear shouts in the Matachine, then a loud noise coming from the street. Fatima becomes pale.

"I can hear the growl of hatred and anger," she whispers. "Something is happening!"

The next second Nour and Gloria pop through the trapdoor, out of breath and with somber eyes.

"The rebels!" Nour says.

"We can't stay here!" Gloria adds.

I feel a great emptiness in my chest, as if it's been punctured, and right then Fatima kneels in front of me.

"Allah has decided," she tells me. "Promise me to grow up a lot when you're in France, Koumaïl. Come, stand up!"

In spite of the terrible, heavy weight that is suddenly crushing me, I obey. Fatima draws me toward her and puts a hand over my head.

"Look how high you come up, Koumaïl. Right to my shoulder!" she says.

I step back to get a better view of the centimeters that separate us.

"If you want to marry me, you'll have to come up to here

at least!" she goes on, her hand suspended in the air above her own head. The challenge is immense!

"How will I ever reach that height?" I moan.

"You will, Koumaïl. If you take good care of yourself."

I look at Gloria, who gathers our blankets, the radio, the kitchen utensils, the catalog, and stuffs them in the gear. Nour is already set to leave; she's waiting for Fatima near the trapdoor.

"Hurry up!" she begs. "The uprising will reach us soon!"

I throw myself at Fatima. She hugs me quickly and then it is all over. We run down the ladder. Downstairs the man who opens the beer bottles is about to lower the iron gate over the bar door.

"Go quickly! It's dangerous!" he shouts.

We are thrown into the street, in the middle of a crowd of fugitives, and the iron gate falls shut behind us. Fatima is dragged away by her mother. As I cling to Gloria, I understand that I am losing Fatima. Just like I lost Emil, Baksa, Rebeka, and the others the night the militia chased us from the Complex. Fear does that. It makes people run in every direction, it sows disorder, and after that you are completely lost.

"Fatima, open your eyes! Look at me!" I shout after her. "You don't even know what I look like! You won't be able to remember me!"

For an instant Fatima fights the crowd that invades the street. She turns back.

Her eyelids resolutely closed, she shouts, "I don't know your face, silly, but I know your heart and the sound of your violin. That I'll never forget!"

chapter twenty-one

IN life nothing goes the way you want. That's the pure and simple truth.

You're separated from the ones you want to love forever.

You want peace, but there are only rebellions.

You want to catch a boat, but you have to climb into a truck.

A truck that stinks of adulterated gasoline, sweat, and wet dogs. A truck that gets stuck in the mud, that tilts over the ruts of mountain roads. A truck that carries other refugees and their overflowing gear.

And what's worse is that no one can understand anything. If God existed, or Allah, he would have a hard time explaining our miseries, right?

Lost in thought, I tell Gloria that I'm fed up with the hazards of life. I'm going to be eleven soon, and all I've known are hurried getaways, rushed goodbyes, and anguish. If it keeps up like this, I tell her, I'm going to jump out of the truck and wait for the soldiers to shoot me.

"Ah, yes?" she says. "And then what?"

"Then I'll be dead, obviously!"

"And you'll be better off, no doubt?"

Through a hole in the tarp that covers the back of the truck, I can see a forest of dense trees pass by. It's darker than a cave in there. If I jump out, maybe I'll be able to live there in hiding for 107 years, like a bear.

"And your mother? Do you think of her?" Gloria whispers. "Do you think she would enjoy hearing that you're dead?"

"My mother doesn't know me. She couldn't care less," I say. "And maybe she's dead too."

"Tsk, tsk, tsk! Jeanne Fortune is not dead. She's alive."

"How would you know? You just tell me stories to force me to live."

Gloria folds her arms over her chest. She thinks a moment as the truck zigzags to avoid puddles. Around us the other refugees try to catch some sleep. They are seated higgledy-piggledy, like rejected merchandise.

"Stay quiet," says Gloria. "I have something very serious to show you."

I'm suspicious. "Do you have more secrets in your box?" I ask her.

"Not in my box, Monsieur Blaise. In my pocket."

I'm angry, but I stay calm. It's raining outside and we are in the middle of nowhere. Honestly, I would rather stay dry by Gloria's side, even if she gets on my nerves.

She searches under her coat and takes out a crumpled envelope. She hands it to me.

"There, open it," she says.

I unfold the paper. In the upper left corner I see the colors—blue, white, and red. And a woman's head. And below, some lines in French. Although I learned the everyday vocabulary in my catalog, I can't read what's written because of the alphabet.

"What is it?" I ask.

"An official document," Gloria whispers like a secret agent. "From the Department of Foreign Affairs. You see that sign up there? It's the emblem of France. Below, it says 'Liberty, Equality, Fraternity.' I had it translated by one of Mr. Ha's friends."

"Oh?"

"Yes indeed. And you know what else it says?" She stops and looks at me so intensely that it gives me goose bumps. "It says that your mother is alive, Monsieur Blaise. Jeanne Fortune in the flesh! It's written here, in black and white! And you know what? She lives at Mont-Saint-Michel. It's official."

I stare with wide eyes. This paper comes from France! It speaks of my mother! It mentions Mont-Saint-Michel! Shaken, I look at the document with such strong feelings that I am about to cry. Then Gloria takes the paper and puts it back in the envelope; we can't afford to lose it.

"Don't worry," she says. "The journey will last longer and it will be more difficult than by boat, but we're on the right track."

Tears run down my cheeks, and I can't decide whether I am sad, happy, or what. My heart has swelled like a sponge.

"And Fatima?" I ask. "Do you think she'll find her aunt in Saudi Arabia? Do you think she'll be happy there with all that sand?"

"*Insha'Allah,*" Gloria answers.

She takes me in her arms like when I was little. She strokes my hair, she rocks me, and her scent of detergent and tea soothes me better than any balm.

"Now go to sleep, little miracle," she whispers. "Tomorrow life will be better."

chapter twenty-two

WHEN I look at page 67 of my atlas, I realize that the Black Sea creates an obstacle. If it weren't there, the Caucasus would be much closer to Europe! But no one can decide to remove an ocean, and no engineer has thought of digging a tunnel with a railroad track under it. This is why we have to make a long detour and cross several countries, several borders, which is dangerous.

I don't know who invented borders, whether it was God or Allah, but I think borders are a very bad idea.

At a border, even when you have an official passport with a photo, you have to jump out of the truck. War demands it. Controls! Barbed wire! Dogs! Cameras! Impossible to go through with a load of famished refugees. So we get out because the driver won't go farther.

"Those of you who are willing to take your chances have to follow this man," the driver says. "He's very familiar with the area and will be your guide."

"And then what?" we ask.

"A truck will meet you on the other side, everything is arranged. Now go!"

We don't have a choice, so we get out of the truck. The guide requests his payment, and we have to pay him in cash down to the last dollar. Only then does he take us to the forest.

We are about fifteen people, walking single file behind this man who opens the way with his flashlight. Around us the night looks like a dark and menacing mouth ready to swallow us. But when you want something badly, you have to suffer in silence. So I walk, twisting my ankles, trying to forget fear, tiredness, and hunger. I am used to it.

It is raining. The mud becomes like glue under the soles of our shoes. I start thinking that it's a waste of time to get clean in the public baths if we have to get dirty in the woods at each checkpoint.

"Tsk, tsk, tsk! Stop whining, Monsieur Blaise, and walk silently," Gloria tells me.

I never thought it would be so difficult to be free. And now, with the humidity and the weight of the gear on her back, Gloria is coughing again. My stomach is in knots when I hear the horrible dog barking in her chest.

"Are there good doctors in France?" I ask.

Gloria catches her breath, hands on her hips. "I don't need a doctor. It's nothing . . . just . . . a coughing fit."

We move ahead between the trees for hours and hours. Our feet slide and roll over stones, dead branches, and other invisible things. To encourage myself, I repeat my everyday vocabulary: *"Helloiwouldlikearoom. Wherecanifindagoodrestaurant? Pardonsiridliketogototheeiffeltower."*

Later on we reach the edge of a village, and our guide tells us to hide in a barn and wait. Our small group huddles together to keep warm, and I finally drift off to sleep.

When I open my eyes, it is daylight. Gloria is talking to the other refugees about what to do. Wait some more? Leave? I ask her where the guide is, and she explains that he has disappeared. He pocketed our money and left without keeping his promise. He's a rat, and now we have to manage on our own.

We leave the barn with tired eyes and enter the village through a street strewn with old tires and empty cans. The first living thing we meet is a yellow-furred dog that comes to sniff at us. As we move ahead, doors open. Children appear suddenly, then women, old people, and they look at us without a word, as if we had fallen from Mars.

At the end of the street, men are gathered. Their faces are the color of wax. They smoke cigarette butts, they spit, and one of them has a rifle tucked under his arm. I can't help but think about the Kalashnikov that killed Fatima's father as he prayed on his rug. I shiver.

"You must be refugees," says the man with the rifle as we reach the group. "Where do you come from?"

We tell him about Sukhumi, the insurrections, the truck, the walk in the forest, and the guide who left with our dollars.

The man sighs. "These guides can't be trusted," he says. "All of them take advantage of people's misery. It's the third time this has happened in less than a month."

The other men nod sternly, and I no longer fear the

rifle. I see that they are just poor peasants who have to deal with the hazards of life.

"We can't do much to help you, but come with us," they say.

They take us to the door of a large hut, where we flock in. It's warm inside, and a pleasant smell of bergamot lingers between the walls. At the back a TV is on.

A woman motions to us to sit down on trunks. She serves us tea in small, decorated glasses, then gives us steaming pancakes with a dish of boiled cabbage. It is the best feast in the world.

"See?" Gloria says, smiling at me. "Never despair of human beings. For every person who lets you down, you'll meet dozens of others who will help you."

I nod. "Right!" I say.

Unexpectedly, the TV shows pictures of Sukhumi. We see the soldiers, the tanks, the planes, and the houses on fire. As we watch, our group of refugees stops eating, and the woman of the house raises the volume so that we can hear the news about our war. I look closely at the screen, hoping to see Fatima and Nour among the fleeing crowd. But everything moves too fast, and at the end a man wearing coveralls appears in front of the camera.

Gloria gets up so quickly that she knocks her tea glass down.

"What is it?" I ask.

She doesn't answer me. She's shaking.

She goes closer to the TV as the man in coveralls speaks into a microphone. The only thing I see is his name written at the bottom of the screen—Zemzem Dabaiev. Gloria turns pale, tears flowing from her eyes.

I come near her. I take her hand. Gloria's hand has never seemed so cold.

"Mother?" I say.

She bends toward me and whispers, "Koumaïl." Then she collapses on the floor of the hut.

chapter twenty-three

WHEN you're only nearly eleven years old, many things are impossible to comprehend, especially about love, war, nationalists, nations' strategic interests—and also Zemzem Dabaiev. It's because of all this that Gloria collapsed on the floor of the hut, but she doesn't want to say anything more about it. When I'm grown up, maybe she'll explain.

"No, not now, Monsieur Blaise. Not now," she says. "We have to continue with our journey by any means possible, and if you ask one more question about Zemzem, I'll wring your neck, is that understood?"

I nod.

We leave the village on board a cart driven by the man with the rifle. He takes us to the bottom of a dark valley that looks as if it had been cut out with an ax from the sides of the mountains. We are finally in Russia. The man says goodbye before turning back to his village, and our group of refugees breaks up, each of us following his or her destiny, *insha'Allah*.

Gloria and I keep going on foot. When we're lucky, we hitchhike in trucks, in dented cars, along roads, rivers, swamps. . . .

We sleep in improvised shelters that don't offer much protection. I am often cold, so I dream of Fatima in the dunes of Saudi Arabia, which warms me up.

By the end the only thing I can say about Russia is that there are lots of hydraulic dams, but very few people.

At the Ukrainian border there is no barbed wire for once. Only armed guards and dogs. Gloria arranges things with the driver of a tourist van that is half empty. He takes our last dollars in exchange for the right to sit with the passengers, who are half-asleep in their seats, their cameras slung around their necks. When you have seen war and bombs, it's strange to see tourists. They would be better off taking pictures somewhere else, I think.

"Let's see if Mr. Ha did a good job," Gloria whispers to me as she hands me my passport.

I turn the pages and look at my photo—a Parisian, clean, well groomed, without lice or fleas. Looks good to me. But I tremble a little when the guard starts inspecting the van.

He's a hulk in uniform, with the thick neck of an ox and dull eyes that remind me of Stambek's. It looks like he forgot his intelligence somewhere too. Our good luck.

"French?" he asks in Russian.

We nod convincingly, but I see that he hesitates when

he looks at the stamps drawn by Mr. Ha. I lean toward Gloria, and without thinking, I blurt out the everyday vocabulary I learned in the catalog. It's a jumble of words that don't make any sense, but the guard doesn't know any better. He may not even know about the Eiffel Tower. He looks at me with his blank eyes, then at Gloria, and again at me.

At last he closes our passports. "Welcome to Ukraine," he says.

We hold our breath until the van goes through the checkpoint and gains some speed.

"Well!" Gloria cries out. "You're a true dictionary, Monsieur Blaise!"

I laugh when I think of my gibberish, but Gloria seems really surprised by my linguistic powers.

"Maybe some French stayed in my memory after the Terrible Accident?" I say. "Maybe I remember a few things subconsciously?"

"Maybe . . . ," Gloria whispers. "In any case, if she could see you, your mother would be proud of you."

I put my head on Gloria's shoulder and close my eyes. Maybe if I concentrate hard enough, I'll be able to remember Jeanne Fortune's face from the depths of my memories. Maybe I'll be able to remember the sound of her voice.

"And my father," I ask, "do you think I knew him? Do you think he carried me in his arms before the Terrible Accident?"

Gloria jerks her shoulder in surprise. "Yes, I think so," she says.

"You think so, but in fact you don't know."

"When one does not know, Monsieur Blaise, one imagines. It's better than nothing."

There is so much mystery surrounding my past and so much uncertainty about my future that it makes me dizzy. I prefer not to think about it. As the van takes the road toward Odessa, I content myself with counting the number of borders we still have to cross before we reach France. There are six, at least. It will take time, but the most important thing is to keep going straight ahead.

chapter twenty-four

IN the railroad freight yard of Odessa, we sleep at the back of a cattle car. The floor is hard and it stinks of cow urine, but I dream that I am lying under the dormer window of the Matachine with Fatima and we are looking at the unchanging stars.

That night our radio and our samovar are stolen. Ukrainian thieves are very silent, and this makes me so sad that I have no courage left.

"Tsk, tsk, tsk!" Gloria says. "The gear is lighter now. In a way, the thieves did me a favor."

chapter twenty-five

THERE are days when I see shadows in Gloria's eyes. Grief does that. Even if she hides it, I know that she thinks of Zemzem, of her five brothers, of Liuba, and of the marvelous fruit in the orchard of her childhood. I have no cure for her. All I can do is keep going without whining, and sometimes I recite the poems of Charles Baudelaire that I learn from my catalog. *"Hommelibretoujourtuchériralamer!"* *Freemanyouwillalwayscherishthesea!*

chapter twenty-six

WE are now in Moldova, in the middle of a totally flat country. Our stomachs have been empty for two days.

We catch sight of a farm. I tiptoe and slip into the hen-house to steal some eggs. I find four of them and get out with my loot.

The farmer appears. He shouts in his language. I run as fast as I can toward the bush where Gloria is waiting for me. My pursuer has long legs and a pitchfork. He catches up with me. I slip. The eggs fall down and break.

The farmer shakes me, pricks me with the fork, but I don't care. I only see the broken eggs, our poor dinner spread in the grass.

The man threatens to call the police. I don't need to speak Moldovan to understand that.

I beg. I cry. I struggle as hard as I can.

Gloria comes out of hiding. She looks pale and seems shaky on her thinned legs. She approaches the farmer and slaps his face in a way that he'll remember until his dying day.

He is so surprised that he lets go of me.

Gloria shouts that it's shameful to abuse a child like that, that he'd be better off hanging himself, old geezer!

I laugh when I see the Moldovan's crestfallen face.

Quickly we leave through the meadows, our stomachs empty, but our dignity and freedom intact. The person who will stop Gloria Bohème, I think, has yet to be born.

chapter twenty-seven

WE stop by the side of a stream and I harvest wild berries that haven't yet ripened. It's our only meal.

When night falls, we settle at the foot of a tree and I ask Gloria to tell me my story.

"Again?"

"Yes, again! With all the details!"

I rest my head against her chest. I can feel the bones of her rib cage under my cheek. She folds me into the lamb-skin blanket and sighs.

"It was the end of summer," she begins. "I lived with old Vassili, my father, the one who gave me the samovar—"

"The one the Ukrainian thieves stole!" I burst out.

"Let's forget about that, Koumaïl. At that time Vassili owned the most beautiful orchard in all of the Caucasus. Apple trees, pear trees . . . acres and acres covered with trees. On one side was a river; on the other, the railroad track."

I lift my head and ask her if she knows what "Zemzem" means in Arabic. She seems surprised.

"Do you mean that you know?" she asks.

"'Murmur of water,'" I say. "Fatima told me. It's nice, isn't it?"

Gloria doesn't say anything, and for a long time we listen to the stream that flows in the darkness. Stars appear between the tree branches. I have a bitter taste of wild berries in my mouth, and my thoughts wander.

"In my opinion, Zemzem has become someone very important," I declare. "That's why he talked on TV. Only important people are shown on TV, right?"

"I don't know," Gloria whispers. "I don't know. . . ."

Her voice falters like a candle in a draft. It's obvious that tonight Gloria doesn't have the energy to tell me my story. I close my eyes. In order to be less afraid of the darkness and the unknown, I call on my ghosts: Vassili and his huge mustache; Fotia and Oleg, with their athletic shoulders; Anatoly, who squints behind the thickness of his glasses; Iefrem, whose hair is curlier than a lamb's; Dobromir, with his angelic smile; and Liuba, who sings with feeling. In my dreams they make a radiant family, a protective circle that surrounds me. They will always be with me wherever I go. Zemzem, too, shrouded in mystery and wearing his combat uniform.

I take Gloria's hand and try to sleep, even though my stomach aches because of the unripe wild berries.

chapter twenty-eight

WHEN we reach Romania, Gloria has totally lost her stoutness. She has coughing fits that scare me stiff. No matter how often she tells me that she is as sturdy as the trees, I don't believe her. But I don't know how to say *"Iamsickandineedadoctor"* in Romanian. Besides, we have no money left for medicine.

So while she rests on a bench, I decide to go to work as we did at Kopeckochka. I go to an open market and sit on the ground in the square. I extend my hand.

Even before I get a first coin, a group of children surround me. We don't speak the same language, but insults need no translation. They tell me to scram, that this isn't my turf. One of them—the leader of the gang—wears a hoop earring and bracelets. He shoves me. When I straighten up, I think of Emil and Abdelmalik: "If you don't fight, you're dead!" Quickly I get to my feet and swing from one foot to the other, fists raised to the level of my face. *Whoosh!* A blow in the air. And *thwack!* A kick! I move and dodge.

And I send an unstoppable uppercut into Hoop Earring's face.

The circle widens. Hoop Earring is on the ground. His nose is bleeding, and I'm sure that he's going to make me pay for that. I get ready to take on whatever comes next, but instead of rushing at me, Hoop Earring starts to laugh.

He laughs so hard as he wipes his nose on the sleeve of his sweater that the others start to imitate him. I don't get it. And then Hoop Earring gives me a thumbs-up—which means "bravo"—and asks me my name.

"Koumaïl," I say, still wary.

Hoop Earring motions for me to follow him, but I point toward Gloria, who has fallen asleep on the bench.

"Mama?" he says, raising his eyebrows.

I nod.

Hoop Earring pauses, then smiles. With his hands he gestures as if he's eating and says, "OK!" It seems that I have a new friend, and I rush to wake up Gloria.

This is how we arrive at the Gypsy camp.

chapter twenty-nine

THE Gypsy camp is a large gathering of caravans set in the curve of a river, not far from a concrete factory that reminds me of the one at Souma-Soula. There are dogs, pigs, chickens, dented cars, tangled-up electrical wires, and laundry drying on lines between the trees. Kids are running around, and women are chatting as they braid baskets. It's clear that people here know how to deal with the hazards of life.

The patriarch of the camp is named Babik. He is a wise man, with a black hat and tattoos on his arms. He has traveled a lot since he was born and speaks every language in the world, better than an encyclopedia.

He invites us into his caravan with Hoop Earring, and we sit on a bench. For a while Babik watches us without saying a word. He screws up his eyes, especially when Gloria coughs, and I wonder what he's waiting for. Just to do something, I show him our passports. That makes him laugh.

"Passports are good for administrations! Put them away!" he says. "I'm only interested in hearing your soul."

"Hearing my soul?"

"Precisely."

"But . . . how?"

Babik folds his tattooed arms. "Can you sing?" he asks.

Pitifully, I shake my head.

"Can you play music?"

I tell him about Fatima's violin lessons and my sad *squeak-squeak* that irritates the ears.

"Well . . . ," Babik sighs. "Can you tell stories?"

I smile. "Yes, that I can do!"

"Fine, I'm listening," he says.

With a patriarch like Babik, it's useless to lie. So I tell the truth about me, about Gloria, Jeanne Fortune, and the train accident. I tell him about the militia, the bell under the canopy, Abdelmalik's death, the war, the poisoned waters of the lake, the glass dust that lines the lungs deep down; I talk about each of the stopping places of our journey, from the Psezkaya River up to the village square where I hit Hoop Earring on the nose, and also about each person that I've met, loved, and lost. The list is long, and my story lasts a good while, but Babik doesn't interrupt me even once.

"Your soul is beautiful, Koumaïl," he says when I finish. "It is brave and as refreshing as dew. But Gloria's is fragile and worn out. She needs to rest."

He turns to Hoop Earring and gives him instructions in Gypsy dialect. Then he looks at me and adds, "You will both sleep in Nouka's caravan. You'll remain under my protection for as long as necessary."

Gloria is too tired even to smile, but I can feel that she is relieved. I thank Babik a million times, and Hoop Earring takes us to Nouka's caravan, at the back of the camp, under a weeping willow.

Nouka is a small woman, neither old nor young, with red hair sticking out of a scarf. She installs Gloria on a worn velvet sofa covered with cat hair.

Nouka's hands are decorated with painted swirls. She speaks Russian as well as Babik does. She was his wife in the past, but not anymore. She is nobody's wife now because she is free.

Nouka also speaks the language of trees, clouds, insects, and earth. Nothing is foreign to her. Not even the secrets that are haunting our minds. I don't have to explain anything about Gloria's soul. She puts her hands on Gloria's forehead, on her throat, and on her chest.

After a while she tells us, "Get out, children. I must take care of this woman."

In my life I have been lucky several times. It's particularly true on that day, in Nouka's caravan under the willow. Because if I hadn't learned to box with Abdelmalik, I wouldn't have punched Hoop Earring's nose, and we wouldn't have met Nouka, and I'm certain that Gloria would have died.

And if Gloria had died, the truth is that I would have let myself die by her side.

chapter thirty

IN the Gypsy camp life is a lot like it was in the Complex. There are drafts, we make heat with whatever is at hand, women do the laundry in large vats, we're wary of the police and of the river cresting. But more than anything, I can play like a child again.

My best friend is Hoop Earring, but there is also Angelo, Titi, Sara, Panch, and Nanosh. Thanks to them, I learn how to fish, to set rabbit traps, to dance, to sing, and to speak Romany. I discover the best places to beg and how to climb the factory wall to lift cement bags, which we give to Babik for the needs of the community.

At night the men make a huge fire. They take their accordions, their guitars, their violins, and they play for hours, like shadows in front of the flames. I listen to them, seated on the ground, as still as a stone. This music makes me wish I could live and die at the same time. Like the hook of a fishing rod, it pulls my heart out of my chest.

"Are you crying?" Hoop Earring asks me.

"No, of course not!" I say as I wipe my tears.

At night in Nouka's caravan, everything is quiet. I sleep in a small corner with the old cat, who shares his fleas with me. During that time Gloria lies on the velvet sofa and fights against illness.

Nouka knows remedies for Gloria's illness. She gathers plants in the woods that she boils in a pot; the smell reminds me of the time when Suki and Maya were taking care of me. If I recovered, Gloria can too, I believe.

"Rest your soul," I tell her. "Get stronger! Don't worry about me. I'm happy here. Babik is a good patriarch."

She smiles with her eyes.

She can hardly talk.

Sometimes she grabs me by the hand and hugs me.

chapter thirty-one

SUMMER comes. I bathe in the river, and Hoop Earring teaches me to dive. We splash the girls; they scream like a flock of frightened birds. I swim underwater until I grow short of oxygen.

I am not afraid to die.

Sometimes Hoop Earring tells me to shush and we tiptoe up to the reeds, above the flat rocks where the girls lie down to sunbathe. We stay there, hidden, like hunters, and when we are lucky, one of the girls removes the top of her swimsuit.

When we go back to the caravans, I feel strange and Hoop Earring doesn't say a word.

One day in August a child is born in the community, and it's a very moving moment for all of us. In total silence Nouka approaches the cradle where the baby is sleeping. She looks at the palm of his minuscule hand. Then, in a strong voice, she makes a prediction.

"The future is beautiful!" she says. "This child will live one hundred years!"

Shouts of joy burst out, and we dance until dawn to celebrate the event.

The next day I ask Nouka to look at Gloria's palm. Nouka bends down, studies Gloria's hand, and whispers something in Gloria's ear.

I stay seated against the sofa, my heart beating madly, waiting for Nouka to leave. I want to know what the future holds.

"So what did Nouka say?"

Gloria strokes my hair. "The future is beautiful, Koumaïl. She says that I'll live as long as necessary."

"Until you're one hundred years old?"

"Until as long as you need me."

Relieved, I smile. "I'll always need you!" I say.

"Tsk, tsk, tsk," Gloria whispers.

She blows me a kiss and tells me to go and play. I run off to meet Hoop Earring at the river. The future really is beautiful! My childish optimism erects a wall between me and any anxiety.

But one day summer comes to an end.

chapter thirty-two

FALL has arrived. The frost freezes the puddles between the caravans' wheels, and the laundry is taken inside. Soon snow will come.

Gloria is better, her strength is back, and the dog no longer barks in her chest. Nouka doesn't need to gather any more plants.

"Gloria's soul is still weak, but you can keep on going now," she assures us.

In the camp everyone is getting ready to go. Gypsies never stay too long in one place. They roam the globe, following the sun and their lucky star. It is their destiny.

"Due south!" Hoop Earring says as he puts aside his fishing gear. He sighs.

I sigh too. South means that we have to go our separate ways and that we will have to be strong to overcome the challenges that lie ahead.

Hoop Earring takes me one last time to the fields to gather the rabbit traps. We collect them one by one. We discover a young weasel that got caught in the last one. She died of exhaustion.

Hoop Earring loosens the trap.

"Be careful, Koumaïl, my brother," he says. "Over there in the west there are many human traps. If you get caught, they lock you in a cage and you die. Just like this."

He places the weasel's body on a bed of grass. We remain silent, standing shoulder to shoulder.

The day we leave, I remove Oleg's violin from the gear and go to see Babik.

"The strings are strange, but you'll know how to play it," I say.

The patriarch strikes the wood of the violin. He pinches the strings.

"It's a very valuable gift, Koumaïl," he says. "Each time we play it, we will think of you. This way we'll keep listening to your soul."

My heart tightens because I think of Fatima.

"If you see a very beautiful girl who comes near you to listen to the sound of this violin, and if her eyes are closed and she sings better than anyone else, tell her that I did not forget her."

Babik smiles and promises to give the message. I kiss his prickly cheeks and I leave in a hurry before I cry.

Then the caravans are attached to cars and the procession begins. Panch, Titi, Sara, Angelo, and Nanosh are gathered against the windows to see me one last time. Gloria and I wave to them. Hoop Earring is not among them, and it's better that way.

Gloria and I start going west quickly, our throats tight, once again seized with the awful feeling that we've left something of ourselves behind. I lecture myself in silence: Come on, don't be sentimental, don't be sad! If you look ahead, the future looks good! And I gather all the hope I have left and imagine the Eiffel Tower covered with snow, and my mother waiting for me near the golden angel of Mont-Saint-Michel.

As we reach the bottom of a hill, I suddenly realize that I walk faster than Gloria. I turn back to her.

"The gear is much lighter now and I've grown a lot," I tell her. "Let me carry it."

She stares at me. "Tsk, tsk, tsk! Are you sure?"

I show her my arms, which have become muscular, and my legs, which are much thicker.

Gloria seems surprised. "Well, now I see that you're right!" she says.

Without hesitation she puts the gear on the ground.

I am so proud to load it over my shoulders. "Soon I'll be as strong as Fotia and Oleg," I declare.

"And you'll have a mustache as long as Vassili's," Gloria adds, laughing.

I laugh too. It's difficult to imagine myself with hairy cheeks.

"Do you think my mother will recognize me?" I ask.

"A mother always recognizes her son, Koumaïl."

I climb the hill easily, and as I reach the top, anxiety grabs me. I wait for Gloria and take her hand.

"Even when I'm all grown up, I'll still need you, right?" I say.

Gloria does not answer. She breathes slowly as she walks, as if she wants to conserve air, and I pray that Nouka wasn't wrong about her future.

"What everyone needs, Koumaïl, is a good place to live. Come on, tell me once more what you know about France."

I walk at her pace along the road. I talk and talk and talk. Each word makes marvelous things appear on the horizon.

chapter thirty-three

THE last memory of my childhood is also the most painful one. It's one I would like to forget, to pluck from my mind the way you pull out a weed in a garden, but it's not possible.

It happens near the Hungarian border, per page 47 of my green atlas. A Greek truck driver dumps us in a large parking lot on the side of a highway. Gloria made arrangements with him, but now he's scared of the customs checkpoint. He no longer wants to hide us behind the curtain of his cab, so he abandons us to our fate, *insha'Allah*.

It is dark and the wind is cold. We go into a service station to take shelter.

I like this place, flooded with light, where anyone can use the toilets for free, drink from the taps, warm up under the electric hand dryer, and admire the candy stand. This is the way it is in democratic and free countries: you come in, nobody asks you anything, and you can stroll quietly between the shelves. If you're tired, you can rest on plastic chairs; no one bothers you.

"Sit down," Gloria tells me. "Don't go anywhere. Pretend you don't exist. I'm going to try to make arrangements with someone else, OK?"

"OK."

Gloria is the queen of making arrangements. First, she inspires confidence. Second, she speaks politely, and people always agree to help us, like the man at the Matachine did, and all the cart, car, bus, and truck drivers who agreed to take us from the Caucasus up to this point.

I look at Gloria as she approaches the counter where the truck drivers are having coffee. From where I sit, I can't hear what she tells them. I only see her smile, knowing they must find her nice and reassuring. The drivers look at her with their big men's eyes. They make room for her at the counter, and one of them orders her a coffee. Afterward they laugh, all of them together, and I can see that Gloria has red cheeks because of the warm coffee.

They talk a long time while I stay on my chair, without moving, as inconspicuous as a ghost. A lot of things go through my head, and I think about what we'll be able to do when we get to France, like eat butter croissants or Camembert cheese. I think about that because I am hungry and I wish Gloria would hurry up, otherwise I'm going to faint.

Finally I see her arm in arm with one of the drivers; they go toward the service station exit. Quickly I grab the gear to follow her, but she motions to me firmly and mouths, "Stay there! I'll be back."

Upset, I put the gear at my feet and I wait. Now I feel uncomfortable, alone in the middle of all the drivers who come and go. To seem more at ease, I take my catalog out of the gear.

I turn the pages so often that they threaten to come loose. I learn by heart each tiny detail about the storming of the Bastille; about Napoléon, who died on Saint Helena; about the Métro and Coco Chanel, the symbol of French elegance. I learn how to use the public toilets and that Eugène Delacroix's head is on the one-hundred-franc bill. I learn the hours of Galeries Lafayette, the big department store, and the top speed of the Paris–Lyon TGV, which is the jewel of the French railway system. I can even list all the castles of the Loire Valley—Chambord, Azay-le-Rideau, Chenonceau, Amboise. . . . But none of it matters if Gloria leaves me in this service station.

What could she possibly be doing with this truck driver? I wonder.

Just as my anxiety becomes unbearable, Gloria appears at the door. She's alone, out of breath, her hair undone, and she has a box of cookies in her hand. I jump to my feet.

"I thought you had forgotten me!" I tell her.

"Nonsense, Monsieur Blaise! You know very well that I would never forget you! You do know that, don't you?"

She gives me the box of cookies and explains that everything is settled. The truck driver agreed to take us to France. He's waiting for us.

"The problem is that there's only one seat in the cab," Gloria says.

"So what are we going to do?"

"Don't worry, we'll cheat a little. I'll stay with the driver in front, and you'll climb into the trailer without being seen."

"Oh?"

"Yes. That's the only way."

Gloria is shaking. I think she looks strange, but it's not the time to dawdle. In agitated gestures she explains what I'm supposed to do.

"Walk behind me, discreetly, up to the truck. The driver must not see you, do you understand?"

"Understood."

"Then slip into the trailer and hide at the back. Don't move from there until we reach France. Do you understand?"

I nod, although the plan doesn't make me happy.

Gloria removes her Jeanne Fortune passport from the gear and orders me to hold on to the rest. If I get cold, I'm supposed to wrap myself in Dobromir's blanket. If I get bored, I'm supposed to look at my atlas.

Gloria puts my passport in my jacket pocket, the one that closes with a button, and she tells me to take good care of it because it's the most precious thing that I own.

"Do you know what to say if someone asks to see it?" Gloria says.

I nod. "I tell the truth: my name is Blaise Fortune and I am a citizen of the French Republic," I say.

"Can you say it in French?"

"Yes. And you?"

"Me, I'll be all right," she says with a wink. "You know that I always manage!"

Gloria holds me tight against her, and I can hear her

heart drumming in my own body as if we were just one. She kisses my forehead and my cheeks with such urgency that it makes me dizzy.

"Come on, Monsieur Blaise, let's go! I told the driver that I needed to use the toilet before leaving. He must be wondering what I'm doing."

She trots to the door and I follow a few steps behind her.

We cross the large parking lot, where lots of heavy trucks are parked. Without losing sight of Gloria, I slip in and out between all the wheels. Finally Gloria stops near a big, muddy truck that has a Spanish license plate. This is it.

She is near the cab, where the driver is waiting. She turns back toward me and points to the rear of the truck. I answer by raising my hand, my fingers making the V sign for "victory." Gloria does the same. I smile and tiptoe off.

When I manage to lift the cargo door, a suffocating smell grabs my throat. I realize that the truck carries livestock, and I can't help thinking that I couldn't be unluckier. But now isn't the time to be choosy.

I go inside and shut the cargo door.

It's so dark that I can't see the tip of my nose; impossible to know exactly what kind of animals I'm dealing with. I hear some scraping, some growling and breathing. I move forward, feeling my way, hurting myself against who knows what. The engine starts just as I knock my head against the back wall.

I put the gear down and sit on the vibrating floor. This is it. We're leaving! I wrap myself in the lambskin blanket, then open the box of cookies. I savor each bite. Because when you're alone in the dark, and it stinks to high heaven, you have to gather strength from everything or you sink into despair.

The sway of the truck rocks me, and I think that Gloria is right when she says that you have to be confident and that you have to follow your path the way the Gypsies do, without worrying about borders.

I tell myself that in twenty-four hours we will be in France. Our ultimate refuge! The country of human rights. The country of the poet Charles Baudelaire.

Yes, within twenty-four hours we will be at the end of our journey and the beginning of a better life. In twenty-four hours I will take Gloria through the peaceful streets of Montmartre. We will walk down the Champs-Elysées and stuff ourselves with butter croissants. And there, at last, we will be free and happy. Forever.

chapter thirty-four

BUT dreams are only dreams, and I did not go to Montmartre. I did not guide Gloria through the labyrinth of small streets. We did not walk down the Champs-Elysées, and no butter croissants were waiting for us on our arrival.

Customs officers who were controlling commercial trucks on the highway near Sarreguemines, in Moselle, discovered me on December 13, 1997, among a cargo of pigs.

As far as I know, they were looking for drugs or smuggled goods. But I was the only contraband they found when they opened the cargo door of the trailer. I was sleeping, my head resting on the gear. I had managed to drift off despite the frightful smell of excrement.

I had had nothing to drink since the service station. My throat was on fire, my lips were dry. The truck driver could not believe his eyes when he saw me and swore loudly in Spanish.

The customs officers pulled me out of the trailer by the

collar of my sweater. I wasn't quite awake, so I didn't have time to think and grab the gear.

I landed on French soil and looked for Gloria.

She was not there.

I rushed toward the driver, begging him to tell me where she was, but he didn't understand anything I said, and I smelled so bad that he kept walking away from me, holding his nose. Then the customs officers pushed him into a car.

"Gloria! Gloria!" I shouted. There was no answer. Only the sounds of traffic on the highway and the wind.

The customs officers dragged me to a van. I fought them as I kept shouting "Gloria," so they handcuffed me. That's how it is when you confront the authorities.

They forced me to climb into the van, and I suddenly thought of the small weasel and of Hoop Earring's warning, but it was too late. I had fallen into a trap set for humans. The door of the van closed on me, and we left the highway. Where was Gloria? Where could she be? I panicked. My head was empty and the steel of the handcuffs was cutting into my skin. I collapsed and cried, *"Helpmehelpme!"*

Later, between two hiccups, I explained: *"Mynameis-blaisefortuneandiamacitizenofthefrenchrepublicitsthepureand-simpletruth."*

I repeated that twice, three times, like a prayer, like a song, but it was as useless as shouting in the desert. The officers sighed. They seemed upset.

I put my head on my knees.

Gloria had disappeared. Maybe she had fallen out of the truck? Maybe she was hiding? Maybe something horrible had happened while I slept with the pigs? I did not know what to think.

I was almost twelve years old, the gear was in the smelly truck, and I was without Gloria in the country of human rights and the poet Charles Baudelaire.

Never in my life had I been so scared.

chapter thirty-five

AT first I saw nothing of France except for walls, doors, gates, dormitories, and corridors.

People talked to me. I didn't understand a single word. They offered me food, but I wasn't hungry. I was sad and I spent my time trying to hold back my tears.

I was waiting for Gloria, you see. I hoped to see her appear at any second, behind each door, around each corner, but she never did.

When your feet ache, you can always pretend that they're somebody else's feet. But when you're filled with sorrow, it's impossible to believe that your heart isn't bursting in your chest. So I stayed in my corner, paralyzed, unable to fight the despair that was eating away at my soul.

chapter thirty-six

I was finally transferred from a holding zone to a shelter, where a man named Modeste Koulevitch came to see me.

He was a white-haired man with a flabby chin that folded over the bow tie of his suit. He looked like an orchestra conductor. I wondered what he was doing there—had he escaped from the national opera like Miss Talia?

"Good morning, how are you?" he said to me in Russian. At last I had someone I could talk to!

I felt so relieved that I burst into tears.

"Well, well, now," Modeste Koulevitch said as he patted me on the back as if I had swallowed something the wrong way.

I wiped my eyes, and he explained that he was an interpreter. He was here to understand my story in order to translate it into French. Translation was his profession.

"What is your name?" he asked.

"My name is Blaise Fortune," I said as I sniveled.

"Yes, that much I know. But your real name in Russian, what is it?"

"I don't have a real Russian name. My name is Blaise Fortune, it's the pure and simple truth."

"All right," he said with a sigh. He took me to an office where there was a computer.

We spent the whole day in front of the screen. I spoke to him in Russian, and he typed the translated words. I told him everything from A to Z like I had in Babik's caravan. But Modeste wanted more details. In a way he, too, wanted to hear my soul.

He stopped me often to wipe his forehead.

"Phew! It's mighty hot in here, isn't it?" he said, pulling on his bow tie. His chin shook like jelly.

Looking at him, I was reminded of what Gloria had told me in the peasant village: never to despair of human beings.

By the end of the day, most of my story was stored in the computer, in black and white. I asked Modeste if he knew where my gear with my precious things was. He didn't. But he promised to inquire, and left.

Thanks to him, the authorities finally understood why Mr. Ha had fixed my passport. He had done a fine job, but it wasn't good enough to fool the experts. That's what brought me to their attention. I argued that it had to be my real passport, since my mother had given it to Gloria the day of the Terrible Accident.

"I agree," said Modeste when he came back, "but the administrators need proof. Your story is so unusual."

I didn't see what was so extraordinary. It was easy to

understand, but the administrators obviously didn't have much imagination. When I talked to them about Vassili's orchard, instead of seeing apples, apricots, and magnificent pears, they wanted addresses, dates, and a lot of numbers.

"Scien-ti-fic proof," Modeste said, striking the table like a hammer with the palm of his hand.

I looked at him blankly because I didn't understand what he meant.

"According to you, this train accident happened in the Caucasus. Where exactly? The Caucasus is so large!"

I shrugged. Sure, the Caucasus was large! One more good reason to let it be and concentrate on easier problems—like finding Gloria and my mother.

"That's just the same!" Modeste said, getting annoyed. "Jeanne Fortune, Gloria Bohème—all of it sounds too incredible to be true. Like a bunch of made-up names."

My mouth dropped open.

Modeste sighed. "All right," he said, seeming sorry.

Nevertheless, after a lot of research and fact-checking, the administrators finally found newspaper clippings and military reports that mentioned the derailment of an express train in the Caucasus.

"A terrorist strike that the nationalists claimed to be theirs, at the beginning of the war," Modeste said to me with a large smile. "The dates don't really match up, but—"

"Is it scientific proof?"

"Somewhat."

"That means that you believe me, then?"

"It means that we'll keep searching."

"To find my real mother?"

"Yes."

"And Gloria?"

Modeste Koulevitch wiped his forehead. He explained that the truck driver had been interrogated. He confirmed that he had taken a woman into his cab in the parking lot at the Romanian/Hungarian border.

"According to him, she was a prostitute," Modeste said.

"He's lying!" I shouted.

"Maybe. In any case, he didn't know her name. He said that she left while he was making a pit stop in Germany."

"He's lying!" I said again.

"It's possible," said Modeste. "But we can't be sure as long as we don't have proof."

I knew that the Spanish driver had lied, because Gloria was not a prostitute, and what's more, she would never have abandoned me in a trailer loaded with pigs. So the mystery remained unsolved and there was nothing I could do but wait patiently in the shelter. But wait for what? I wondered.

"Well," Modeste said, "wait until we know who you really are and whether France can keep you or not."

According to the laws of the French Republic, I was considered an "unaccompanied foreign minor." Modeste Koulevitch explained that France could not let everybody enter its borders under the pretext that it was a country that stood for human rights. Inquiries had to be made, otherwise it would be too easy for children in lots of war-torn countries everywhere to make the same request.

"You understand, don't you?" Modeste asked.

I did not understand but said "OK" to be left alone.

* * *

I had to tell my story many more times and give many more details and fill out millions of forms. Modeste perspired enormously. He said that I was going to drive him crazy if I kept repeating that I was a citizen of the French Republic and that it was the pure and simple truth.

And I was waiting for Gloria.

I stayed posted near a window in the shelter, my eyes on the horizon, even though the horizon stopped at the bottom of the opposite buildings.

I looked up at the sky. I tried to keep calm. I told myself that wherever I was on this earth, the sky was always the same. It was a constant, like the stars, the sun, and the planets. And I imagined Gloria watching the same sky, a thought that gave me comfort.

Then one day Modeste Koulevitch read Article 20 of the convention to me, concerning the rights of children: it meant that I had obtained the protection of the state.

"As long as we can't find someone who knows you, and we don't know where you come from exactly, we're stuck," he added.

I was sent to another shelter, near the town of Poitiers, and there I was enrolled in school. That was the law also. I thought this was a good idea because otherwise I would have kept waiting for Gloria, and despair would have killed me.

chapter thirty-seven

IN France school isn't anything like the university for the poor, or like Fatima's school, where everyone prayed to Allah on a rug. In France no one would ever teach you about the different cuts of beef, or the list of martyred saints, or the rules of poker. Never. First you have to learn the language. And this time it wasn't like the phonetic sentences of Mr. Ha.

In my class we were eleven "unaccompanied foreign minors." Most of the others came from Morocco or Tunisia; others were black like Abdelmalik. They had left their families at page 90 of my green atlas; that is, in Africa. Others were born in different parts of the world, like Colombia or the Philippines. I learned that there are many dangerous places for children on our planet.

We didn't need to talk to understand one another; each of us had gone through the hazards of life—hunger, border crossings in the middle of the night, the fear of patrols, the noise of Kalashnikovs—and had known distress that rips your guts out when you're alone in the world. Our memories and our feelings acted like cement: we were as united as the bricks of a wall. This was very important because no one can live without human warmth.

The picture that I've kept from that time shows all of us together: Malik, Anissa, Fatou, Samy, John-Aristide, Sabado, Wema, Jamal, Leandro, and Prudence. Behind us is our teacher, Mrs. Georges, who smiles with beaming pride. Thanks to her, within a few months we became adept at conjugating verbs.

Time went by.

I turned thirteen and still lived in the Poitiers shelter, under the protection of child social services.

My gear was never found. It was definitely lost, so I couldn't show the official document concerning Mont-Saint-Michel and my mother. I thought that maybe the pigs—those omnivorous animals—had eaten the pages of my atlas and my catalog. But I would never know.

I was finally able to recite the poems of Charles Baudelaire with barely an accent: "Free man, you will always cherish the sea!" I was able to construct complex sentences and use adjectives, and the list of France's kings held no more secrets. But I wasn't officially French, and Jeanne Fortune was nowhere to be found. When Modeste Koulevitch visited me from time to time, he said things were status quo.

"What does that mean?" I asked.

"It means that there's nothing new, that nothing has changed, Blaise. You're not French or anything else."

"OK."

This was nothing new to me; I was used to being a ghost. A draft.

As for Gloria, her disappearance remained a mystery and my heart was broken. I feared that she might be dead because of the dog in her chest, or that she might be caught in a trap for humans somewhere in Europe. The laws of this world are stricter for adults, for the very reason that they are not minors, and Mrs. Georges always looked gloomy when I spoke of Gloria.

"Maybe she was deported," she said.

"That means sent back to the Caucasus?"

"Yes."

"Even if she was sick?"

"Yes."

I thought that was unfair, and I was terrified at the idea of never seeing Gloria again. Many times I had dreamed of the peaceful life we would have; I had imagined the wonderful reunion with Emil, Stambek, Fatima, and all the others, and I was despondent.

At night I bit my pillow so that no one would hear me cry.

My only hope was Nouka's prediction. Gypsies are very good at divining things, and I clung to the idea that Gloria could not die as long as I needed her. I preferred to believe that she had found Zemzem again, or that she had taken shelter in the cottage in Vassili's orchard. I imagined her happy, boiling water in a brand-new samovar. I saw her climbing a tree or driving a truck, laughing with her brothers, who had all come back alive from the war. I made up stories to make reality more bearable, just as Gloria had taught me.

In 1999, as I turned fourteen, the computer in our class was linked to the Internet. According to Mrs. Georges, it was a very important event, and she was happy to initiate us into new technologies that would become our passport to the new millennium.

"With this tool," she said, "you'll know everything about anything!"

Our eyes shined because we were all searching for something or someone in this vast world of ours. Jamal asked if it was possible to learn about people who had been lost in the Mediterranean. His brother had drowned during their trip to Europe.

Mrs. Georges looked sad. "With this tool you'll know *nearly* everything about anything," she corrected herself.

She explained how to use the Internet, and I decided to make my own inquiry to get out of the status quo.

The first word I entered in the search engine was "Gloria."

Results:
- concentrated milk trademark
- American actress, dead a long, long time ago
- Latin words of a Christian prayer
- lots of restaurants and hotels

Not a trace of *my* Gloria, even when I added "Bohème," which sent me to a European region and to a song and to a poem by Arthur Rimbaud.

As sad as ever, I entered a second request: "Jeanne Fortune." This was even worse because no one seemed to have that name, either at Mont-Saint-Michel or anywhere else in France.

Finally I entered "Zemzem Dabaiev." At last something popped up—newspaper clippings in Russian saying that Zemzem was a warlord, a terrorist, a bloodthirsty monster who was armed to the teeth and who had killed many innocent people. I was sure they were mistaken, that they weren't talking about the same person, because Gloria's Zemzem wasn't a monster. Gloria's Zemzem had saved people; he had run to get the tanker truck. He wouldn't hurt a fly.

Upset, I abandoned the computer. I went to see Mrs. Georges and shouted that I was disappointed with the new technology. What good was it to be modern if the millennium didn't offer me a little bit of hope? I demanded.

"Lies, that's all there is in there! Lies!" I cried.

I slammed the classroom door and stormed out, a ball of rage forming in my stomach.

I sat on a low dividing wall at the back of the courtyard that surrounded the shelter, near the athletic field. I was fed up with everything, with my friends, even with Modeste Koulevitch and Mrs. Georges and her kindness. What I wanted was Gloria. She was the only one who knew the truth! She was the only one who could help me find my mother, the only one who could bring the scientific proof that I was French. Even more important, she was the only one who could soothe my distress by taking me in her arms.

I cried a long time, hitting my heels against the wall, then, unexpectedly, I felt a presence behind me. When I turned, Prudence was looking at me.

"What do you want?" I snapped. "My picture?"

I was in a foul mood.

Prudence smiled. She came near me.

"If I sit here, you're not going to bite me, are you?" she asked.

I shrugged and she sat down.

I was surprised because Prudence was the quietest and shyest girl in the class. I didn't know much about her except that she came from Liberia, a country that borders the Gulf of Guinea. I remembered that it was on page 91 of my green atlas.

She remained silent for a long while. Suddenly she asked me if I wanted to play a game.

"A game? What game?" I asked.

"A contest."

"What kind of contest?"

"A contest of misfortunes."

I stared at her inquisitively.

"It's simple. We each mention something unhappy that happened in our lives," she explained. "The winner is the one who has had the most misfortunes."

I thought this was funny. "OK," I said.

And we played.

Misfortune for misfortune.

For a long time we stayed sitting side by side on the wall in front of the athletic field.

We revealed everything about ourselves, starting with our oldest memories. And the pure and simple truth is that Prudence won by far. What had happened in only thirteen years of her life was unbelievable! A list to make the hair on your head stand on end—massacres, fleeing through a hostile jungle, venomous stings, beheadings, and scars on her arms to prove torture. By the end of the game, my mouth was agape. She made the victory sign with her fingers, and tears ran down my cheeks because I was reminded of the last time I had seen Gloria in the parking lot.

Prudence handed me a tissue.

After that we became inseparable. Not really in love, as when I was little. Just inseparable.

chapter thirty-eight

BECOMING inseparable from someone makes you happy. All it takes is meeting the right person—whether by chance or, if you are a believer, because Allah makes it happen.

Prudence was the right person for me, and I began to tell myself again that I was lucky. Because if I hadn't fallen asleep with the pigs, if the customs officers had not apprehended me, if Article 20 had not existed, and if Prudence's family had not been hacked to pieces, she and I would never have come to Poitiers, and we would never have met.

chapter thirty-nine

THE year 2000 was over. I turned fifteen, then sixteen and seventeen.

Apart from the times when I thought of Gloria and got depressed, I was adjusting to my new life. In the morning I got a freshly baked baguette, the smell of Mrs. Georges' coffee filled the classroom, and there were fireworks on the Fourteenth of July and the annual Tour de France.

I was getting used to living in peace and I was getting ready to take the high school exam.

I walked the streets, hand in hand with Prudence, waiting to be of legal age so I could obtain my French citizenship and become a person rather than a ghost.

It happened officially on December 30, 2003. I remember it clearly because it was very cold on the square of the city hall. Modeste Koulevitch and Mrs. Georges came with me, and Prudence was there too. They each kissed me as if I had won a sports event, as if I'd broken a world record at the

Olympics. I was holding an ID card and a brand-new passport in my hand.

"This is a wonderful day!" Mrs. Georges said, crying.

And Modeste Koulevitch patted me on the back again and again because he was so happy for me. The laws of the republic had recently changed: France still stood for liberty, equality, and fraternity, but many new amendments made it increasingly difficult to obtain official papers. The new immigration policy, based on fear, as always, had made it that way. But I had gotten my papers. I could breathe.

We went to a restaurant to celebrate, and Mrs. Georges ordered a glass of champagne. Then she asked me what I was going to do with my newfound freedom.

Prudence leaned against my shoulder. She knew my plans because I had told her about my dreams. We smiled at each other.

chapter forty

PRUDENCE went to sleep. I did too, my head leaning against the bus window. The driver had to shake us awake to tell us that we had arrived.

It was low tide. The huge parking lot was almost empty, flooded with gray puddles. Seagulls were flying in all directions, crying in the January sky. In front of us the Abbey of Mont-Saint-Michel seemed surreal, planted in the sand, surrounded by a veil of fog that came from the sea.

Prudence took my hand.

Heavy drops began to fall as we reached the fortified city. Our hoods over our heads, we ran to take shelter under the awning of a store.

"My gosh," Prudence said as she looked at the torrential rain running over the cobblestones.

I had come with every intention of questioning the inhabitants about my mother. One after another, if necessary! We had looked in the telephone book, and there weren't many, maybe about forty in all. It seemed easy enough to do, but once we were there, walking the narrow lanes, I felt indecisive.

Fried-food smells floated in the damp air. The souvenir shop sold countless plastic knickknacks, all of them made in China. It was a tourist trap, but I wanted to buy something, regardless.

When we came out of the shop, the rain had stopped and Prudence took me toward the stairs leading to the summit.

I raised my eyes. In between the mossy roofs, the statue of the golden angel was watching us.

The view was magnificent from the top. The rain had cleared the sky; big, dark clouds hovered over the horizon, and the immense spread of the bay glistened in the sun.

I looked at the landscape for a long time. Thoughts were churning in my head and I grew dizzy. I had to move away from the edge and sit on the stairs with my eyes closed.

Prudence was quiet. She waited. I guess when you've seen your family massacred in the suburbs of Monrovia, nothing can surprise you. She understood the pain that I felt at finally being at my birthplace, without a mother or a father to tell me who I really was.

The dizziness passed. I opened my eyes. Behind me the angel was shining in the sun. I started to laugh.

"What's so funny?" Prudence asked.

"I don't know." I took a deep breath and contemplated the abbey. "Come on, let's go."

Prudence didn't comment about the many bus hours we

had spent to get here, or the savings we had used to pay for the trip, or my fickleness. She followed me and we headed down.

While we were looking out onto the amazing panorama from the top, I had realized that being at Mont-Saint-Michel and finding Jeanne Fortune weren't essential. I didn't have to question the forty people who lived here to confirm what I already knew. The most important thing was to find Gloria.

chapter forty-one

WHEN you reach legal age and you're officially a French citizen and the everyday vocabulary is at your finger-tips, you're able to lift mountains. Even if they're in the Caucasus. Even if it takes a lot of time. Even if you some-times lose courage. Even if you feel that it's a waste of time and that it would be easier to look for a needle in a haystack.

It took me eighteen months and dozens of letters, phone calls, and e-mails. Finally I received a letter from the French Embassy in Tbilisi, Georgia, in the Caucasus.

The letter is in my suitcase. It says:

Dear Mr. Blaise Fortune,

We believe that the person you are looking for might be here. But the situation is delicate. You will need to come in person to the following address.

Etc, etc.

So on a morning in July 2005, I am at Charles de Gaulle Airport, my heart beating madly, the memories of my childhood rushing through my head, with the little made-in-China knickknack that I bought at Mont-Saint-Michel in my pocket.

Now it's time to board the plane, and I can't help thinking of a Charles Baudelaire poem that says, "It is time! Let us raise the anchor!"

The gate attendant checks my passport, smiles at me, and wishes me a safe trip.

chapter forty-two

I spend the first night in a hotel in the center of Tbilisi. Unable to sleep, I stand in front of the open window. It is stifling hot. I observe the lights, the traffic of cars, the facades of the illuminated cathedrals and mosques. Is it here that I lived with Gloria in the Complex? I wonder. Or was it in another town? I don't recognize anything, and I wait impatiently for sunrise with a sort of fever that brings me close to nausea.

After almost nine years of being away, what I know of the Caucasus is that it hasn't changed much. Officially the war is over, but there are still rebel fighters, Kalashnikovs, shifting borders, and refugees who slip in and out through the valleys. From time to time there are attacks, kidnappings, people who disappear. It is the kind of place that no one can understand. Yet people live here. They breathe, they walk in the streets, they work, drink, eat, even have fun.

At last the sky is clearer, and dawn brings some coolness.

I take a shower, shave, button my shirt, and look at myself in the bathroom mirror. I can't help thinking that I'm as clean as the day I came out of the puliba. I'm a real French-man, rid of lice and fleas. Now I wonder if I've become a stranger on the soil where I spent my childhood. And I wonder if Gloria will recognize me.

I leave the hotel, my throat tight. The hospital address is written on a piece of paper folded in my pocket. No need to read it again, I know it by heart.

Dr. Leonidze greets me. He is a soft-spoken man, elegant, and he speaks Russian with a bit of an accent. The French Embassy notified him about my visit, and he offers me a cup of tea in his office.

It is only eight in the morning. The sun shines through the window. I perspire in my clean shirt.

"Before I take you to her room," Dr. Leonidze says, "I have to tell you that she has not said a word in seven years."

The cup of tea shakes in my hand.

"She has been here for seven years?" I ask.

Dr. Leonidze nods. "When she arrived here, she was in very bad shape."

"Was she . . . was she coughing?"

"Yes, with a serious infection of the respiratory tract. At first we thought it was tuberculosis, but the illness is more likely the result of chemical poisoning. These days her con-dition is stable."

I put down my cup and wipe my sweating forehead.

"During all these years," Dr. Leonidze goes on, "we didn't know her name or where she had come from, so we called her *outsnobi khali*, "the unknown" in Georgian. Some more tea?"

I shake my head. What I want now is to see her.

"If she is the person I'm looking for, I . . ."

I don't know how to finish my sentence. Actually, I don't know what will happen if it is my Gloria who is here. I feel like I'm floating in a state of weightlessness. The doctor finishes drinking his tea and cleans the two cups.

"A few months ago a TV channel came here to make a documentary about the hospital," he explains. "They filmed our patients, and we allowed them to show *outsnobi khali*. Shortly after a man came. He said he recognized her. According to him, her name is Gloria Vassilievna. Some articles appeared in the newspapers about her."

He wipes his hands on his smock.

"Come," he says, "I'll take you to her."

I get up. We leave his office and walk down corridors. The elevators are out of order, so we have to use the stairs to go to the third floor. All I hear are the sounds of our footsteps on the tiled floor and my heart drumming in my chest.

Dr. Leonidze stops in front of a door.

"The man who thought he recognized our patient wanted to see her, just as you do this morning," he adds. "He talked to her, and Gloria Vassilievna started to cry. It was the first time that she showed any emotion. But she still did not say a word. So don't expect too much, you understand?"

"I understand."

My legs can hardly carry me. I don't even think to ask him the name of the man who made Gloria cry. I only see the doctor's hand on the doorknob.

chapter forty-three

I see someone, from the back only, seated in front of a window. I enter.

The sunlight is intense. I squint, walk around the bed, and come closer. The woman's dark hair is gathered behind her head, and a few locks are loose at her temples. I approach her. I can see her profile now, the line of her nose, the curve of her cheekbones. A bomb explodes in my chest: a bomb that irradiates my entire body and splinters me into a million pieces.

It's her. It's really her. It is *my* Gloria.

She turns her face toward me. Her gaze is like a dead star, a black hole. I lean forward. My hands fall to my sides.

"Gloria?" I say.

My mouth is as dry as a desert.

"It's me, Gloria. It's Koumaïl."

The dead stars of her eyes focus on me. No sign of life. Nothing. Emptiness.

I try again. "It's Koumaïl. I came back. Can you see? It's me . . . Monsieur Blaise."

It seems as if something is happening. A vague glimmer lights up her expression. I kneel down in front of her because I don't have the strength to stand any longer. My throat constricts, but I have to talk to keep this glimmer alive.

"You remember . . . nearly eight years ago you told me to climb into the back of a truck driven by a Spaniard. It was in the parking lot at the Hungarian border. Do you remember? You told me not to move. And I did as you told me, Gloria. I stayed with the pigs, in the dark."

As I talk, I see Gloria's eyes come back to life. Each word is like a puff of wind over dying embers.

"When I arrived in France, you were gone. I was alone and I didn't know where you were. I . . ."

In spite of myself, I start crying. I put my hands on her knees and I can feel her warmth. She is as thin as when we were in the Gypsy camp, but she is here in front of me, alive! Except for her expressionless face, she hasn't changed much.

"It's me, Koumaïl!" I say again. "I've grown up. I've changed, of course. Do you recognize me?"

She lifts her left hand and brings it close to me with hesitation, as if afraid to get burned or bitten. I stay motionless, on my knees; suddenly, an image of Fatima's father as he was killed praying on his rug pops into my mind. I wouldn't want to die now for anything.

Gloria's hand touches my cheek, as light as a bird on a twig. She brushes my skin; she feels the shape of my face.

Her mouth opens and lets out an indefinable sound, something like the cry of a wounded animal. Then she starts sobbing, unable to stop. Life has returned to her eyes, and they are devouring me. It feels almost like a fairy tale, when the princess wakes up after sleeping for a hundred years.

She grabs my hands.

"Nouka was right!" I sob. "I knew it! You could not die! As long as I needed you, you could not."

Gloria opens her arms. I throw myself against her, just like when I was little, trying to find again her detergent-and-tea smell.

Gloria strokes my hair. She rocks me.

After so many years of silence, she utters words in a broken voice that puts fire in my heart.

"I was waiting for you, Koumaïl."

Gloria is unable to say anything more that morning, but it doesn't matter. We have all the time in the world ahead of us now.

"Isn't that right?" I say to Dr. Leonidze once we are back in his office.

The doctor shakes his head slowly and his eyes are like two sad orbs in the middle of his face.

"Not all the time in the world, Mr. Fortune. A few weeks, a month, maybe two. No more than that, I'm afraid."

I look at him without understanding.

"But you told me that her condition was stable!"

"Stable doesn't necessarily mean healthy, Mr. Fortune. Gloria's lungs have been eaten away by chemical products. We were able to slow down the progression of the disease, but she is terminally ill."

A blazing rage rips my chest. I get up and come close to the doctor.

"You don't know anything!" I shout at him. "I'm taking her back with me to France! There are better doctors over there! They'll know what to do to save her!"

Dr. Leonidze puts his hands in his pockets. He sighs, resigned.

"I strongly advise against such a trip, Mr. Fortune. She is not strong enough. It would take a miracle to save her."

I look at him with a triumphant smile.

"I came at the right time, then. I *am* that miracle!"

chapter forty-four

I rush back to Gloria's room. I knock over the bedside table.

"Come on, let's go!" I say. "I'm taking you away from this hospital. Where's your suitcase?"

Gloria shakes her head. She doesn't have a suitcase. What would she put inside it? I wonder. Except for the clothes provided by the hospital, she owns nothing.

"Fine!" I say. "Even better!"

I open the small closet, where a sweater and a pair of pants are hung, and I throw them on the bed.

"We'll go to the French Embassy. They'll give you a visa, you'll see. They'll understand that it's urgent. I'm a French citizen, don't forget! I have an official passport! I'm free, and no one will keep me from taking you back with me to Paris!"

I get hold of a pair of shoes at the bottom of the closet while I keep talking fast, shaking from the excitement.

"You aren't staying one more second in this room!" I tell

her. "These doctors are useless! That's why your health is declining! I'll take care of you, you'll see! You'll feel better! Because the truth is that you're as sturdy as the trees!"

With the closet empty, I start to fold the clothes, but Gloria's eyes catch mine. She gives me a look that forces me to be quiet. She does not move from her chair. She smiles with a mysterious sweetness, just like the Mona Lisa.

"What's the matter?" I ask.

Gloria pats the bedspread with her hand, as if saying, "Sit down and stop this foolish agitation." But I'm obsessed; I want to take her far away from here, to keep her far from death. I've waited almost eight years, and I haven't moved heaven and earth to abandon her now.

"We'll talk on the plane," I say. "I'm going to find a bag for your things."

"Tsk, tsk, tsk," Gloria whispers.

And her smile wavers.

Suddenly I'm drained of energy. I go sit on the bed, close to her.

It isn't as hot now, as the sun is coming through the window on a slant. I can hear cars honking in the street.

Gloria and I look at one another for a long time, and I try to decipher what it is that she can't tell me. Almost crying, I recognize that it would be foolish to leave Georgia.

"OK, you're right, we'll wait," I say. "There's no hurry after all."

Gloria smiles again now. She seems relieved.

"Would you like to go out for a short walk?" I suggest.

* * *

It is afternoon, and Gloria walks slowly. We wander aimlessly, under sculpted balconies and laundry hung out to dry in windows. Dogs pass by, sniffing the walls. I realize that Gloria stops often to regain her strength.

After a while we sit under a tree and share the bottle of water that I brought from the hotel. There is so much to say that I don't know where to begin.

We remain silent, our eyes directed to the river at the bottom of the hill. Birds are singing, insects are buzzing; if it weren't for the shells of buildings destroyed by the war, you'd think the Caucasus was a peaceful region.

"When we lived in the Complex, was it here?" I ask. "I mean in Tbilisi?"

"You remember?" Gloria says, surprised.

"Of course! I remember everything from there on."

I describe to her my first memory, with the laundry and Sergei, who shaved my head.

"And before that?" she asks.

"Before that you told me everything. About Vassili, Zemzem, the Terrible Accident . . ."

Gloria sighs. Her eyes search for something in the landscape, then settle back on me.

"You've grown so much, Koumaïl. Are you happy in France?" she asks.

How do I answer this question? In a way, yes, I am happy. I have a roof over my head; I am never famished or cold; I get financial help to complete my studies at the university; I often walk in Montmartre; I drink cool beer on café terraces with friends; I laugh; I go to the movies when I have enough money; and above all, there is the love that I share with Prudence. But a profound sadness has stayed with me each day of my life, an inconsolable sorrow that feels like a hole where my heart should be.

I look down to pick a blade of grass and roll it between my fingers.

"I didn't find my mother, you know," I say.

When I look up again, Gloria is staring at me. Her expression and the pallor of her face scare me.

"Do you want to go back?" I say, worried.

She motions that no, she does not want to do that. She leans back against the tree trunk, lost in thought or contemplating the sun playing in the leaves.

"It's time that I tell you your story, Koumaïl," she says finally.

"My story? You told it to me a million times. I know it by heart! Don't tire yourself."

"Tst, tsk, tsk. It's a new version."

"Oh?"

"Come here, like in the old times. I've been waiting nearly eight years for this moment."

I've never been able to disobey Gloria. So I stretch my legs out on the grass and I put my head on her stomach. In spite of her weight loss, her middle is still comfortable, and it soothes me to feel Gloria's breath on my face.

"You have to promise me something," she says before she begins.

"What?"

"Not to interrupt me."

I promise as she strokes my forehead. Then I close my eyes to concentrate on her voice.

I don't say a word. I listen to my story. The new version.

chapter forty-five

"IT was the end of summer," Gloria begins. "In 1984, to be precise."

"At that time I was twenty and the Caucasus was part of the Soviet Union. Russians, Georgians, Ingushetians, Armenians, or Abkhazians, we all lived under Moscow rule. It was the hazard of history, and nobody would have thought that this would change for a long time to come.

"My father, old Vassili, was Russian. He and Liuba, my mother, had settled in Abkhazia to work in an orchard. It was not his orchard: in spite of his suspenders and his huge mustache, Vassili was a simple laborer. He possessed nothing but the strength of his arms and his six children. You remember them, don't you? Fotia and Oleg, with their athletic shoulders; Anatoly, who hid his eyes behind thick glasses; Iefrem, whose hair was curlier than a lamb's; Dobromir, with his angelic smile. And me, his only daughter."

I smile as I hear the names of the members of this

ghostly and ideal family that has lived in my imagination since childhood.

"That summer Zemzem arrived at the orchard. He came from Chechnya, a republic farther north. He was as poor as we were, but he had received an education. He was very handsome; we fell in love at first sight. We walked under the trees, we spoke about a thousand things. I admired everything about Zemzem: his vitality, his intelligence, his ideas, his knowledge. So when some months later I realized that I was expecting his child, I felt happy. Happy like never before."

My heart jumps in my chest and my breathing accelerates. I don't dare open my eyes, in case Gloria stops talking.

"On December 28, 1985," she goes on in a voice slowed with emotion, "I gave birth to a magnificent boy. Everybody had gathered at the house—Liuba, Vassili, and my five brothers. Zemzem was proud and filled with wonder. He put his hand on his son and said that it was a miracle.

"This child, it was you. And we called you Koumaïl."

I can no longer breathe. I am paralyzed.

In the silence that follows, a drop of water falls on my forehead. I jerk. When I open my eyes, I see tears running along Gloria's cheeks.

Breaking my promise, I whisper, "It was me? You mean that—"

Gloria puts a finger on my lips. Her whole body is trembling, so I keep my questions to myself.

"We were happy together for a few years," she goes on. "But things changed suddenly around 1989, when the power of the Soviet Union declined. The many different peoples of the Caucasus started their claim for independence. It was a bit like having put a lid over boiling water for fifty years. When you lift the lid, you burn yourself.

"Zemzem was ready to act. He gathered men around him to organize for the liberation of the smaller enslaved republics. He spoke well and with such conviction that many workers wanted to follow him. Starting with me! We wanted to start a revolution. We wanted people to live freely, on their own land. We wanted people to speak their ancestral language, to practice their own religion, their own culture. Zemzem was ready to take big chances to make that happen, but I did not realize it. I attended the meetings, I listened to the speeches, and I was excited.

"With a small group of volunteers, we met in secret in a shed at the back of the orchard. I saw the weapons, the chemical products, all the war equipment, arrive. Zemzem often said that our revolution could not be a peaceful one. With fervor he taught us how to make bombs.

"You should have seen us manipulating cans and toxic powders without any protection. We were totally fearless. We were so young!

"Vassili and Liuba were worried, and so were my brothers. Vassili said our family was Russian and that it was none of our business to interfere with the business of Abkhazia, Chechnya, or Georgia. We were just small farmers, apple pickers! We had to leave politics and weapons to others! But I was too much in love to listen to my father.

"One night, at the end of the summer of 1991, I went with Zemzem and the others along the railroad track. Everything was ready; we put our explosives on the tracks.

"In the morning, when the express train appeared on the horizon, I realized the gravity of our actions. Fear overcame me. I begged Zemzem to defuse the bomb. He refused. The express train was carrying Georgian soldiers, and according to him, they were our enemies. I shouted that there were also civilians on the train, women and children. I couldn't change his mind. The train was getting nearer. I didn't know what to do.

"The bombs exploded.

"There was a terrible commotion.

"Zemzem and the others made the V sign for 'victory' and left. But I could not.

"The train was on fire, people were screaming, so I came closer. I heard the calls of a woman. I slipped into a ripped-open car and I crawled between the torn seats.

"She was in a ball in one corner, blood all over her face. She held a baby against her breast. I bent down. It was too late; the baby was dead. I tried to drag the woman out, but she died before I got too far. I stayed there, close to her, crying, not knowing what to do.

"And then, in the middle of the mess, I found her suitcase. Inside there was a lambskin blanket, a radio, a poetry book, French cigarettes, clothes, a violin. There was also a wad of American dollars and two French passports—hers and the baby's. I took the suitcase. Farther away I noticed a large canvas military bag that the force of the explosion had emptied. I transferred the contents of the suitcase into it; I lifted the bag onto my back and got out of the car.

"Outside, help was arriving, including Vassili and my

brothers, who tried to put out the fire with the tanker truck. I met the horrified stare of my father and he understood what I had done.

"That very evening I told Zemzem that I did not want to participate in his group's actions anymore, that it was criminal and cruel. We had a very violent argument. You were there, Koumaïl. You cried when you heard us fight. Zemzem calmed down and took you on his knee and asked if you thought that he was a criminal. You said no, of course. Zemzem held you tight in his arms and said, 'And your mother? Don't you think she is a coward?' You cried again, not understanding what was happening. You were only five years old. Even I was terrified."

Suddenly I start to suffocate. I rise on my shaky legs. I lean against the tree trunk. I open my mouth, trying to breathe again. A jumble of thoughts swirl through my mind. I feel like howling and I am unable to define my feelings. Is it anger I feel? Disgust? Relief? Fear?

After a while Gloria whispers, "I have to finish the story, Koumaïl. Then you'll be able to judge."

I set myself down at the foot of the tree. I have no strength left, and I listen, my head in my hands, to Gloria's weak voice.

"The war had been hatching for a long time between the Abkhazians and the Georgians," she goes on. "After the attack the region fell rapidly into serious political problems, and a price was put on Zemzem's head. He had no choice but to go underground. Of course he wanted us to come with him. When he looked at you, he seemed angry. He said that he would make a proud soldier out of you, a hero. You, a child! So I made a decision.

"I went to see Vassili and Liuba. They gave me the samovar, some food, and the green atlas that you loved so much to look at. My brothers kissed you and bid me farewell. Fotia put a piece of paper in my hand, with the name and address of a man he knew in Sukhumi, a trusted friend who worked at the Matachine and who would be able to help me if I needed to leave the Caucasus.

"That same night Vassili took us in his truck to the neighboring town. He left me there with you. My old father's heart was broken, but he couldn't forgive me for having taken part in the bombing, and I understood that he didn't want to see me again.

"I was afraid that Zemzem would try to pursue us, afraid that the Georgian militia would link us to him, afraid of everything. It became clear in my mind that nobody must know that I was Zemzem Dabaiev's wife, and nobody must know that you were his son. We had to get a new identity, hide the truth, break off the ties that united us, even the ties between you and me. It was a matter of life or death.

"We survived a full year going from place to place. I don't want to remember some of the people I met then, but I also found others who were kind and helped us. And all my hopes rested on the two French passports I had stolen. I believed that one day they would save our lives.

"That's the time I began to make up stories. You were so small! How could you overcome the ordeal of such a grim reality? I didn't want you to keep the memory of a terrorist father. I didn't want the burden of the dead people on the train on your shoulders. I didn't want you to suffer the same heartbreaking experience I had when I left my family. I wanted your life to be beautiful, filled with hope and light. So I made up the story of your birth and your childhood. I imagined a more romantic past for you.

"Every night I added some details, some new events. I opened the gear and used its contents to give weight to my lies. The book, for instance, was by a French poet who lived in Russia. His name was Blaise Cendrars. I got the name Jeanne from one of his poems. 'Fortune' was just a brand of cigarettes. I didn't feel I was lying to you. My only concern was to protect you."

I am motionless under the tree in the summer heat of Tbilisi. My head is still in my hands, and my heart is pumping noisily. Above my head the sun has moved and is over the river now. I am not hungry or thirsty. I do not feel anything but total bewilderment.

Gloria is exhausted, and I think that she is scared of what is to come.

"And Mont-Saint-Michel?" I manage to ask.

Gloria sighs. "When Mr. Ha falsified our passports, he erased the original names so that no one could link us to the woman and her baby who died in the Terrible Accident. He noticed that the pictures in the catalog filled you with wonder. He's the one who thought of Mont-Saint-Michel. There is your true story, Koumaïl."

I look at the Caucasus sky, its small clouds and its magnificent blue. I try to gather my thoughts, without success.

I have the feeling that I could stay here for a hundred years without saying a word; that I could take root in this dry soil, become a stone, or crumble into dust.

Later an insect lands on my cheek. I chase it away with my hand, and this mechanical gesture brings me back to life.

"I'm your son. Your real son . . . ," I whisper.

Gloria suppresses a sob. "Do you remember the list of precious things?" she says.

I nod.

"You always wanted to know what Zemzem had given me. And I refused to answer. Now I can tell you that he gave me the most precious of all the gifts. You."

I kneel in the grass to look at the person who has just spoken these words. It is Gloria. My Gloria. My mother! My mother, who cries silently and trembles as if she were cold, even though it is so warm outside. She lied to me, I think. All along, she lied to me.

But all I say is, "Deep down I think I always knew it."

chapter forty-six

THAT evening I realize that I don't know where I stand. I need to be alone and think. Gloria is exhausted. I feel relieved to take her to her room.

Before I leave the hospital, I go back to Dr. Leonidze's office. I ask him who the man was who recognized Gloria from the TV documentary. He explains that the man refused to give his name.

"It happens frequently here." He smiles. "The war happened not that long ago. We all have our wounds."

I nod and say that I will be back tomorrow.

I walk in the city for hours without bothering about the recommendations the embassy gave me concerning safety at night. I am not afraid. I feel out of touch.

Back in my hotel room, I sit by the window, in front of the table, with a notebook and a pen. I make a list, in French, like Mrs. Georges taught me to do when faced with a difficult situation:

1. My real name is Koumaïl Dabaiev.

2. I was born on December 28, 1985, in an orchard in Abkhazia that is situated in the Caucasus, per page 68 of my green atlas.

3. My mother is Gloria Vassilievna Dabaieva.

4. My father is Zemzem Dabaiev.

5. I am Russian on my mother's side, Chechnyan on my father's. I became a French citizen through a lie.

6. Jeanne Fortune does not exist.

7. Blaise is the name of a poet. Fortune is a cigarette brand.

8. A woman and a baby died in the express train, killed by a bomb. The bomb was made by my mother and placed under the train by my father.

9. I am the son of two criminals.

10. Vassili is my grandfather; Liuba, my grandmother. I have five uncles. Are they still alive?

11. Zemzem is still alive. He has to be the one who recognized Gloria on TV. Is he still in Tbilisi?

12. Gloria lied to me.

13. Gloria abandoned me in the truck filled with livestock.

14. Why?

I put down my pen and look at the list. I am wiped out. Drained.

I totter to my bed and collapse.

The next morning I wake up, wondering if I dreamed it all. I feel like someone who's coming out of a long coma. The world around me doesn't look like it did yesterday, and yet it is the same sky, the same sun.

After a warm shower I telephone Prudence. It's eight o'clock in Paris, and I imagine her in our small studio, still in a nightgown, in front of her cup of coffee. In half an hour she will lock the door to go to work at the flower shop where she earns the better part of our rent. She will come back home tired but will spend the evening studying because in September she's taking an exam to become a teacher.

She's happy to hear my voice. She was waiting for my call.

"So?" she says.

"I found Gloria."

"How do you feel, Blaise?"

"OK."

"And how is she?"

"Very sick. She could die soon. I don't think she could make the trip to France. I need to stay here with her."

"Of course."

"I really wanted her to meet you, and for you to get to know her."

"I wanted that too," Prudence answers. "Show her the photos."

"I will."

There is a short silence. I hear a strange echo on the line.

"I'll tell you everything when I get back," I say. "The whole truth about Blaise Fortune."

"OK." Before hanging up, she adds, "I love you, Blaise."

chapter forty-seven

DR. Leonidze welcomes me on the threshold of the third-floor room. He pushes me gently out the door, but I still have time to see tubes in Gloria's nose and her pale face on the pillow.

"Come," Dr. Leonidze says, pressing me on. "Let's talk first in the corridor. It won't take long. Then I'll leave you alone with her."

The corridor is depressing in spite of the decorative prints and the pastel paint. The doctor puts his hand on my shoulder.

"Her condition took a turn for the worse," he explains. "Last night we put her under respiratory assistance."

"The tubes?"

"Yes, the tubes."

He explains the seriousness of her condition, the terrible deterioration of her lungs. He tells me that she is conscious, that she can talk, but not for too long. He begs me to treat her gently. If need be, I can push the button by her bedside and a nurse will come.

He leaves me and I enter her room.

Her eyes are open. Her arms are resting alongside her body.

"Koumaïl." She smiles. "I was afraid you would not come back."

"Shhh," I whisper as I sit close to her. "Try not to speak too much."

"Tsk, tsk, tsk. You can't listen to doctors. We have very little time left."

A knot tightens in my throat.

"Don't say silly things, you're going to get better," I murmur.

To ease my anxiety, I show her the gifts I brought from France. First my passport and my French ID card.

"Official papers," I say. "With holograms that can't be falsified. Even Mr. Ha couldn't fake these."

Gloria smiles on her pillow.

"I'm so happy for you," she says. "That's what I always wanted—to be able to give you a future. Here it wasn't possible. In France it is. It's a good country."

I put my papers aside. I sigh.

"Maybe, but it's not *my* country."

"It is now! It is your country."

"I don't know."

I take out the second gift. It's the plastic knick-knack that I bought at Mont-Saint-Michel—a snow globe where you can see the mount with the abbey and the statue of the angel. When you shake it, snow swirls around. It's pretty.

"I bought it the day I thought I would find my mother again. Take it," I say.

Gloria takes the snow globe in her hands. She looks at the mini island inside, surrounded by the sea and sailboats.

"It's a marvelous place to be born," she says.

"Yes, but I wasn't born there."

"Is that so important?" Gloria asks. "When the story is nice, you feel like believing it, don't you?"

"I don't know."

I take out the third gift: the photo album that I prepared with Modeste's and Mrs. Georges' help. All the pictures that we could gather are glued in there. The first one dates back to my arrival at the shelter in Poitiers. As Mrs. Georges pointed out, I don't look too happy. Then there are pictures of my class, taken year after year; my birthdays, where I smile a little more. From page to page you can see me grow up. In the last ones I'm with Prudence, and our pictures are taken in front of the Paris monuments—the Eiffel Tower, Notre Dame, the Arc de Triomphe, Sacré-Cœur, the Louvre and its glass pyramid. . . .

"This is Prudence Wilson," I say. "She comes from Liberia. We've been inseparable these last six years. Now we live together in a small studio. She wants to become a teacher. Do you like her?"

"Beautiful, really beautiful," Gloria answers, unable to hold back her tears.

I close the album. Gloria takes my hand and squeezes it tight.

"I would have loved to come with you to France all those years ago," she says. "I knew it would be difficult, but I thought I could do it. Then the worst happened and it tore my heart out."

She squeezes my hand.

"When I told you to climb into the trailer of the Spanish driver's truck, I was terrified by the idea of being separated from you. But it was the only way to give you a chance. A child who arrives alone in France, even with a false passport, can make it."

"You mean that . . . that you knew what was going to happen?"

"No, I did not know! It was a gamble, Koumaïl! I was hoping with all my heart to be able to reach France with you. But I couldn't lie to myself: an adult with false papers, someone hunted in her country of origin for terrorism, has very little chance of getting across all the borders. What was the best thing to do? Staying with you in the Caucasus would have put both our lives in danger. Do you understand?"

I look at her, scared, overwhelmed, lost.

"I don't know," I almost cry out.

"Look at me, Koumaïl. At that time I was already sick, you remember. I was constantly afraid of dying, even when I told you I wasn't. I had to find shelter for you, far from the war, far from Zemzem, before anything happened to me."

I rub my face with my hands, torn between revulsion and despair.

"The truck driver said that you left while he was making a pit stop in Germany," I tell her.

"You believed him?"

"No. But what happened?"

"I think he became afraid of the checkpoints." Gloria sighs. "When we reached Germany, he told me he had to get some gas. There was a line at the pump, and he gave me money to go and get some coffees. I trusted him. I left the cab. When I came back with the two cups, the truck was gone."

Gloria's face freezes in a grimace of pain. She begins to shake. I lie down next to her in spite of the catheter, in spite of her frailness, and she holds me tight.

"I thought I'd lose my mind from sorrow, Koumaïl," she says. "I tried to make my way toward France on foot. But I was arrested and sent back to the Caucasus. The only thing that kept me alive all these years was the thought that you were free and safe in France. Your life is over there now! You're French. The future is all yours."

I don't say anything.

"Remember what we used to say?" she goes on. "Walk—"

I put my finger on her lips. "Shhh. You have to keep quiet, to rest," I tell her. "I have so much information to absorb that I think I'm about to explode. I'll come back tonight, OK?"

She nods.

"I want to keep you as long as possible," I say when I get up. "I still need you."

I put the snow globe and the photo album close to her on the bedside table. I am about to leave but change my mind. I still have three important questions to ask.

"Is Zemzem the one who recognized you on TV?" I ask.

Gloria looks up toward the ceiling. She hesitates. Then she nods.

"Is he in Tbilisi?"

Again she nods.

My last question is not really a question, but I have to say it.

"Now can I call you Mother for real?"

Gloria nods three times—three times for "yes."

I leave the room and shut the door in a hurry. I hardly take three steps in the corridor before I hear her sobs.

chapter forty-eight

THREE weeks go by, in the sultry heat of summer.

Thanks to Dr. Leonidze, I rent a small room near the hospital, a tiny and cool room on the street level of a building that is threatening to fall down in ruins. My window opens over a paved courtyard where the kids of the area gather. I watch them play for hours, falling prey to a nostalgia that I cannot chase off.

Gloria's health has ups and downs. Some days I find her rested, alert, and we go for a walk. Other times she doesn't have the strength to do anything. So I sit by her side, enjoying the moment.

She asks about France, about my studies, about the thousand projects that Prudence and I have in mind. She wants so many details that she wears me out. When she's satisfied, I'm the one who asks questions. That's how we try to fill the gap that time has created between us.

And always our conversations end in the same way.

"Are you mad at me, Koumaïl?"

"No, I'm not mad at you, Mother."

"Sure?"

I kiss her. She kisses me. Before I leave for the night, I read to her one of Blaise Cendrars's poems, where he talks about Russia, the Trans-Siberian, and little Jeanne of France. Prudence bought the book in a Paris bookstore and mailed it to me. Gloria's favorite part is where little Jeanne constantly asks, "Tell me, Blaise, are we far from Montmartre?"

I read in French, and, in a whisper, Gloria repeats, *"Diblaisesommenoubienloindemonmartre?"* *Tellmeblaisearewefarfrommonmartre?*

Then one evening when I go to the hospital, Gloria has all sorts of tubes around her, an IV in one arm, and an oxygen mask on her face, and Dr. Leonidze informs me that she has lost consciousness.

A machine has been installed near her, a machine that breathes for her.

"It's the end," he tells me.

I remain speechless.

"If you want to spend the night with her, you can."

chapter forty-nine

I am seated in an armchair, next to Gloria, facing the machine that breathes for her. Night has come over the city. The air is mild and I open the window because I don't like the smell of the medications.

I write in my notebook.

The time of miracles is over. My mother, Gloria Vassilievna Dabaieva, is only forty-one years old, and yet she is dying. I fear that I drained her of what little energy she had left by reappearing in her life, forcing her to remember the past. Dr. Leonidze says that it is not so. He says that her illness dates far back. He says that if she was able to survive until now, it was because of me. He may be right. Maybe Gloria waited to see me again, as Nouka predicted. She was keeping so many secrets inside her! It was her burden: a kind of invisible gear that kept her going, kept her moving forward. Now that she has unburdened herself, Gloria Bohème is free to cross the last border.

I stop writing.

My mother's eyelids are closed. She reminds me of Fatima, who refused to look at the world, to see the violence in it. What has become of her? And Emil? And Stambek, Maya, Suki, Hoop Earring, Mrs. Hanska, of all those whose paths I crossed? In life there are so many promises never kept. . . .

I write some more.

Is there a difference between a lie and a made-up story?

The lights of the machine blink in the dark, and I have no answer to my question. The only thing that I am sure of is that Gloria loved me.

I put down my notebook and get up to lean on my elbows at the window.

The wind is balmy. The town is spread out under my eyes, its many lights like the reflection of a starry sky. People bustle back and forth. They follow their destiny, coping with life's hazards, worries, sorrows, and the Kalashnikovs in a Caucasus that continues to waver between war and peace. And here I am, almost twenty years old. I have a father who may be waiting for me in this town, a girlfriend in another town, and a heart that is spread wide between the pages of the atlas.

I turn around. Gloria is nothing but a body stretched under a sheet now. I guess that she will not see the light of another day.

I come close to her. I lean down to kiss her forehead. In spite of the immense sorrow that overwhelms me, I smile and squeeze her hand. Among all the things she gave me, I know there is a foolproof remedy against despair: hope. So as my tears run down my cheeks, I promise her that I will live my life the way she taught me to. I will always walk straight ahead toward new horizons.

About the Author

anne-laure bondoux
has written several novels in varied genres for young people
and has received numerous literary prizes in her native
France. Among her previous novels published by Delacorte
Press is *The Killer's Tears*, which received the prestigious
Prix Sorcières in France and was a Mildred L. Batchelder
Honor Book in the United States.